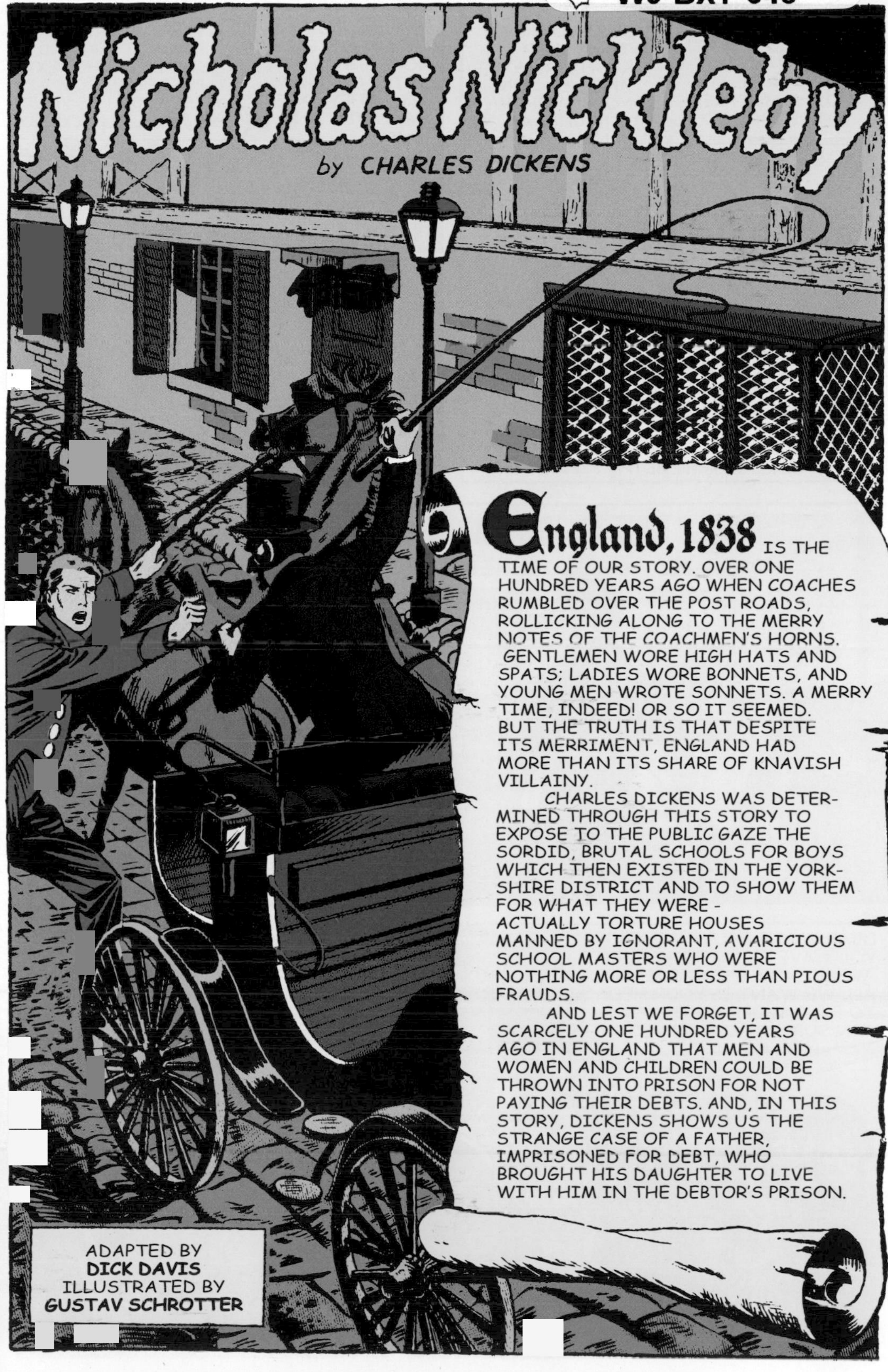
Nicholas Nickleby
by CHARLES DICKENS
England, 1838 IS THE TIME OF OUR STORY. OVER ONE HUNDRED YEARS AGO WHEN COACHES RUMBLED OVER THE POST ROADS, ROLLICKING ALONG TO THE MERRY NOTES OF THE COACHMEN'S HORNS. GENTLEMEN WORE HIGH HATS AND SPATS; LADIES WORE BONNETS, AND YOUNG MEN WROTE SONNETS. A MERRY TIME, INDEED! OR SO IT SEEMED. BUT THE TRUTH IS THAT DESPITE ITS MERRIMENT, ENGLAND HAD MORE THAN ITS SHARE OF KNAVISH VILLAINY.
CHARLES DICKENS WAS DETERMINED THROUGH THIS STORY TO EXPOSE TO THE PUBLIC GAZE THE SORDID, BRUTAL SCHOOLS FOR BOYS WHICH THEN EXISTED IN THE YORKSHIRE DISTRICT AND TO SHOW THEM FOR WHAT THEY WERE - ACTUALLY TORTURE HOUSES MANNED BY IGNORANT, AVARICIOUS SCHOOL MASTERS WHO WERE NOTHING MORE OR LESS THAN PIOUS FRAUDS.
AND LEST WE FORGET, IT WAS SCARCELY ONE HUNDRED YEARS AGO IN ENGLAND THAT MEN AND WOMEN AND CHILDREN COULD BE THROWN INTO PRISON FOR NOT PAYING THEIR DEBTS. AND, IN THIS STORY, DICKENS SHOWS US THE STRANGE CASE OF A FATHER, IMPRISONED FOR DEBT, WHO BROUGHT HIS DAUGHTER TO LIVE WITH HIM IN THE DEBTOR'S PRISON.
ADAPTED BY DICK DAVIS
ILLUSTRATED BY GUSTAV SCHROTTER

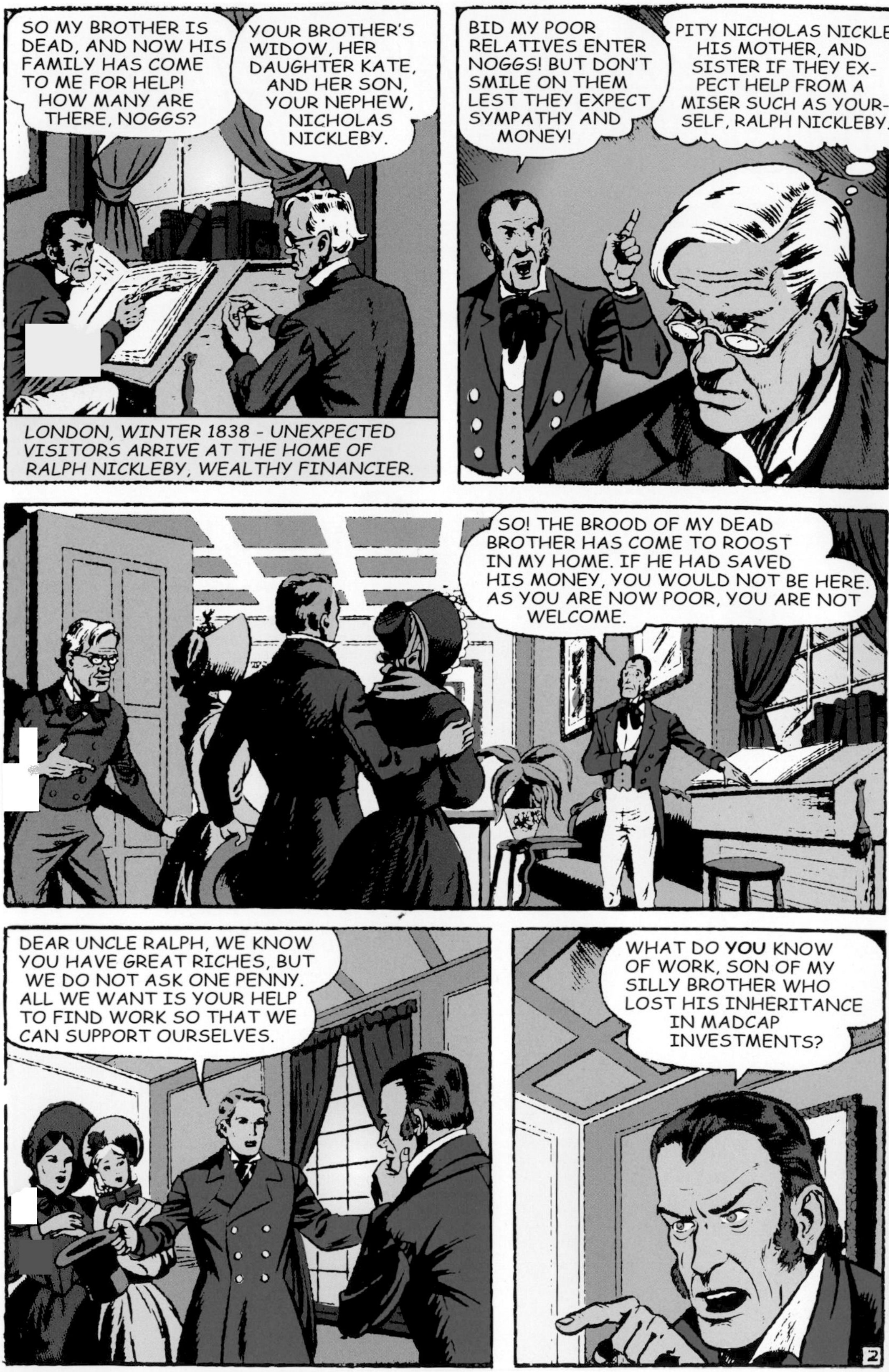
SO MY BROTHER IS DEAD, AND NOW HIS FAMILY HAS COME TO ME FOR HELP! HOW MANY ARE THERE, NOGGS?
YOUR BROTHER'S WIDOW, HER DAUGHTER KATE, AND HER SON, YOUR NEPHEW, NICHOLAS NICKLEBY.
LONDON, WINTER 1838 - UNEXPECTED VISITORS ARRIVE AT THE HOME OF RALPH NICKLEBY, WEALTHY FINANCIER.
BID MY POOR RELATIVES ENTER NOGGS! BUT DON'T SMILE ON THEM LEST THEY EXPECT SYMPATHY AND MONEY!
PITY NICHOLAS NICKLEBY, HIS MOTHER, AND SISTER IF THEY EXPECT HELP FROM A MISER SUCH AS YOURSELF, RALPH NICKLEBY.
SO! THE BROOD OF MY DEAD BROTHER HAS COME TO ROOST IN MY HOME. IF HE HAD SAVED HIS MONEY, YOU WOULD NOT BE HERE. AS YOU ARE NOW POOR, YOU ARE NOT WELCOME.
DEAR UNCLE RALPH, WE KNOW YOU HAVE GREAT RICHES, BUT WE DO NOT ASK ONE PENNY. ALL WE WANT IS YOUR HELP TO FIND WORK SO THAT WE CAN SUPPORT OURSELVES.
WHAT DO YOU KNOW OF WORK, SON OF MY SILLY BROTHER WHO LOST HIS INHERITANCE IN MADCAP INVESTMENTS?
2

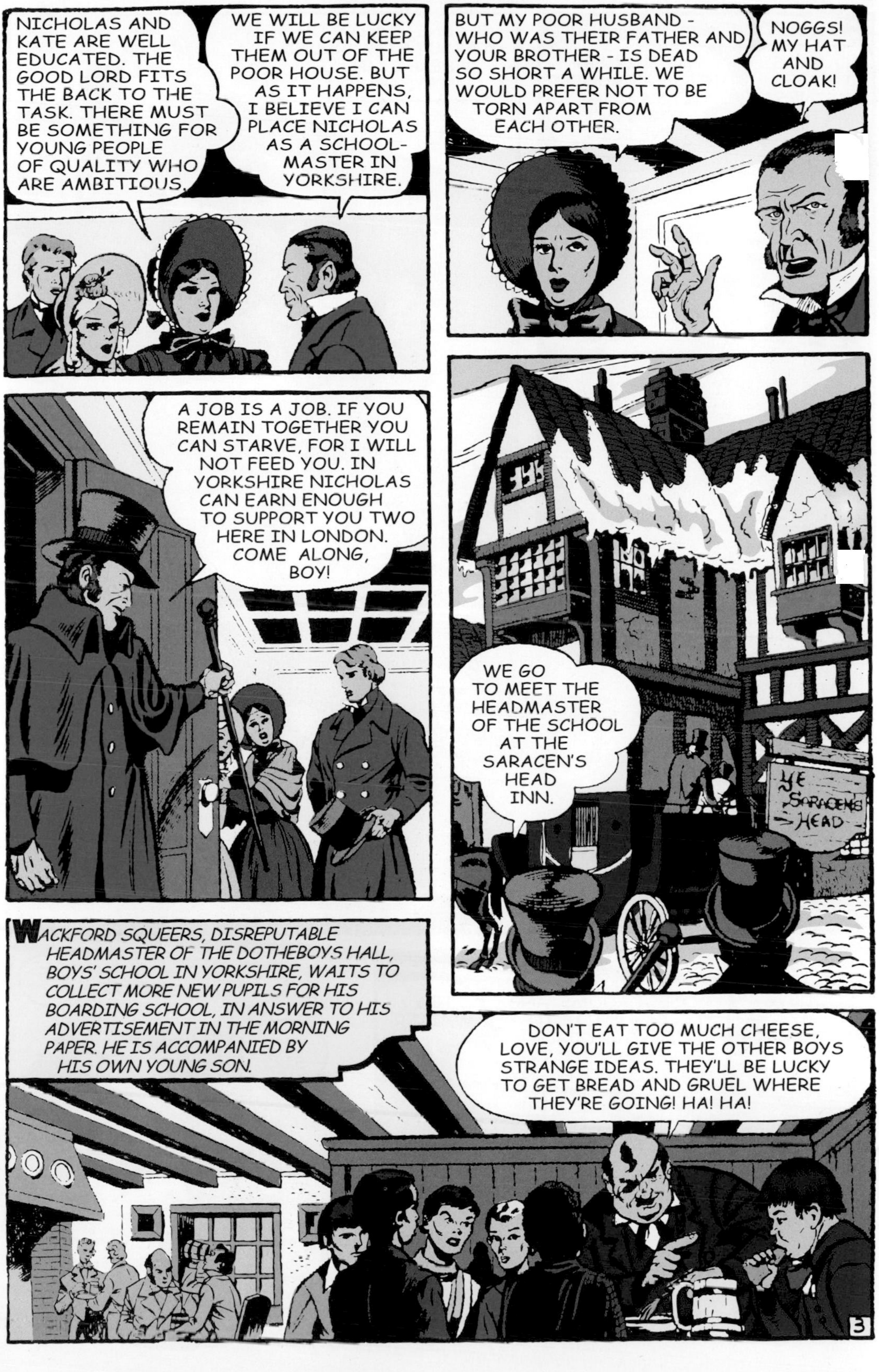
NICHOLAS AND KATE ARE WELL EDUCATED. THE GOOD LORD FITS THE BACK TO THE TASK. THERE MUST BE SOMETHING FOR YOUNG PEOPLE OF QUALITY WHO ARE AMBITIOUS.
WE WILL BE LUCKY IF WE CAN KEEP THEM OUT OF THE POOR HOUSE. BUT AS IT HAPPENS, I BELIEVE I CAN PLACE NICHOLAS AS A SCHOOL-MASTER IN YORKSHIRE.
BUT MY POOR HUSBAND - WHO WAS THEIR FATHER AND YOUR BROTHER - IS DEAD SO SHORT A WHILE. WE WOULD PREFER NOT TO BE TORN APART FROM EACH OTHER.
NOGGS! MY HAT AND CLOAK!
A JOB IS A JOB. IF YOU REMAIN TOGETHER YOU CAN STARVE, FOR I WILL NOT FEED YOU. IN YORKSHIRE NICHOLAS CAN EARN ENOUGH TO SUPPORT YOU TWO HERE IN LONDON. COME ALONG, BOY!
WE GO TO MEET THE HEADMASTER OF THE SCHOOL AT THE SARACEN'S HEAD INN.
YE SARACENS HEAD
WACKFORD SQUEERS, DISREPUTABLE HEADMASTER OF THE DOTHEBOYS HALL, BOYS' SCHOOL IN YORKSHIRE, WAITS TO COLLECT MORE NEW PUPILS FOR HIS BOARDING SCHOOL, IN ANSWER TO HIS ADVERTISEMENT IN THE MORNING PAPER. HE IS ACCOMPANIED BY HIS OWN YOUNG SON.
DON'T EAT TOO MUCH CHEESE, LOVE, YOU'LL GIVE THE OTHER BOYS STRANGE IDEAS. THEY'LL BE LUCKY TO GET BREAD AND GRUEL WHERE THEY'RE GOING! HA! HA!
3

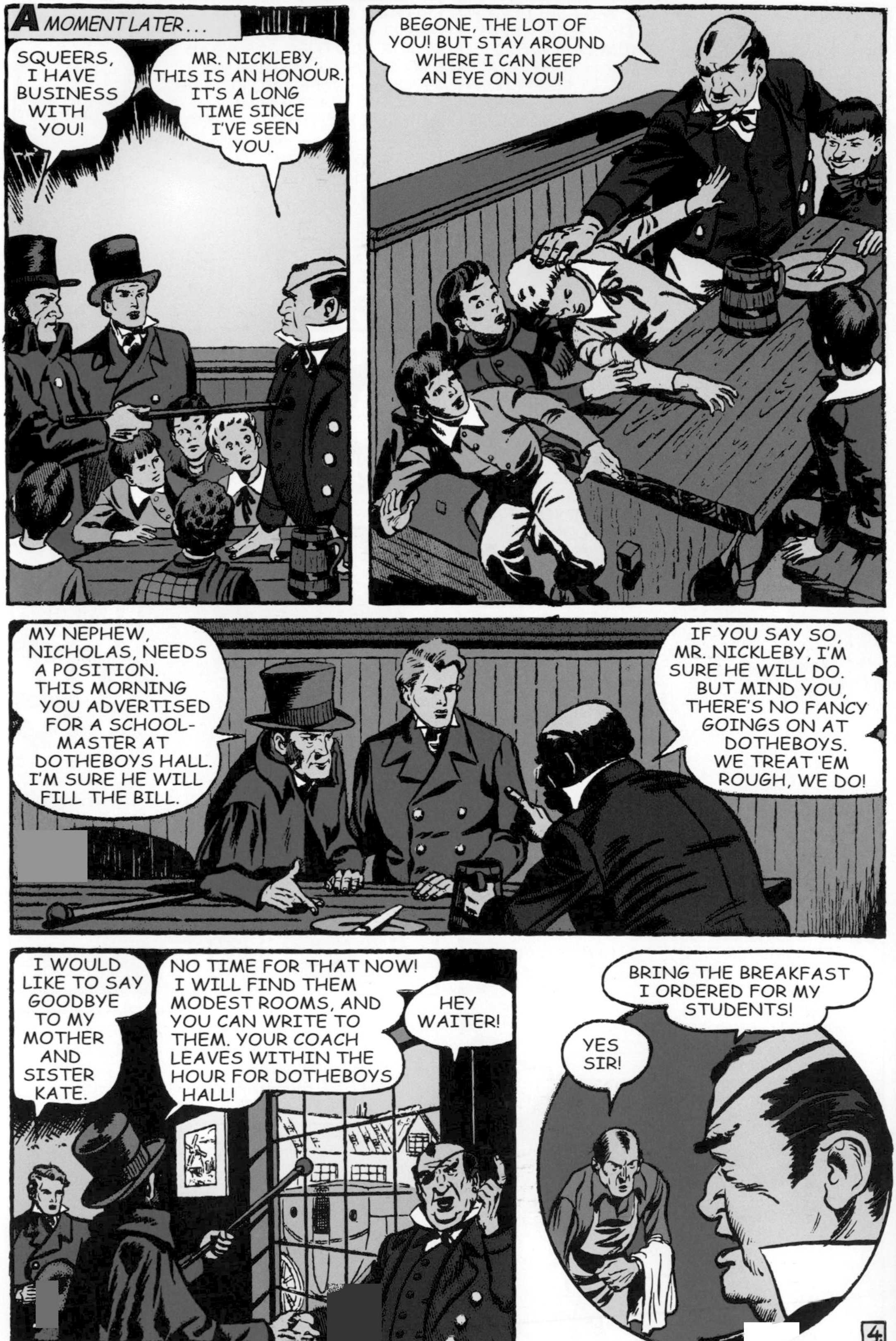
A MOMENT LATER...
SQUEERS, I HAVE BUSINESS WITH YOU!
MR. NICKLEBY, THIS IS AN HONOUR. IT'S A LONG TIME SINCE I'VE SEEN YOU.
BEGONE, THE LOT OF YOU! BUT STAY AROUND WHERE I CAN KEEP AN EYE ON YOU!
MY NEPHEW, NICHOLAS, NEEDS A POSITION. THIS MORNING YOU ADVERTISED FOR A SCHOOL-MASTER AT DOTHEBOYS HALL. I'M SURE HE WILL FILL THE BILL.
IF YOU SAY SO, MR. NICKLEBY, I'M SURE HE WILL DO. BUT MIND YOU, THERE'S NO FANCY GOINGS ON AT DOTHEBOYS. WE TREAT 'EM ROUGH, WE DO!
I WOULD LIKE TO SAY GOODBYE TO MY MOTHER AND SISTER KATE.
NO TIME FOR THAT NOW! I WILL FIND THEM MODEST ROOMS, AND YOU CAN WRITE TO THEM. YOUR COACH LEAVES WITHIN THE HOUR FOR DOTHEBOYS HALL!
HEY WAITER!
BRING THE BREAKFAST I ORDERED FOR MY STUDENTS!
YES SIR!
4

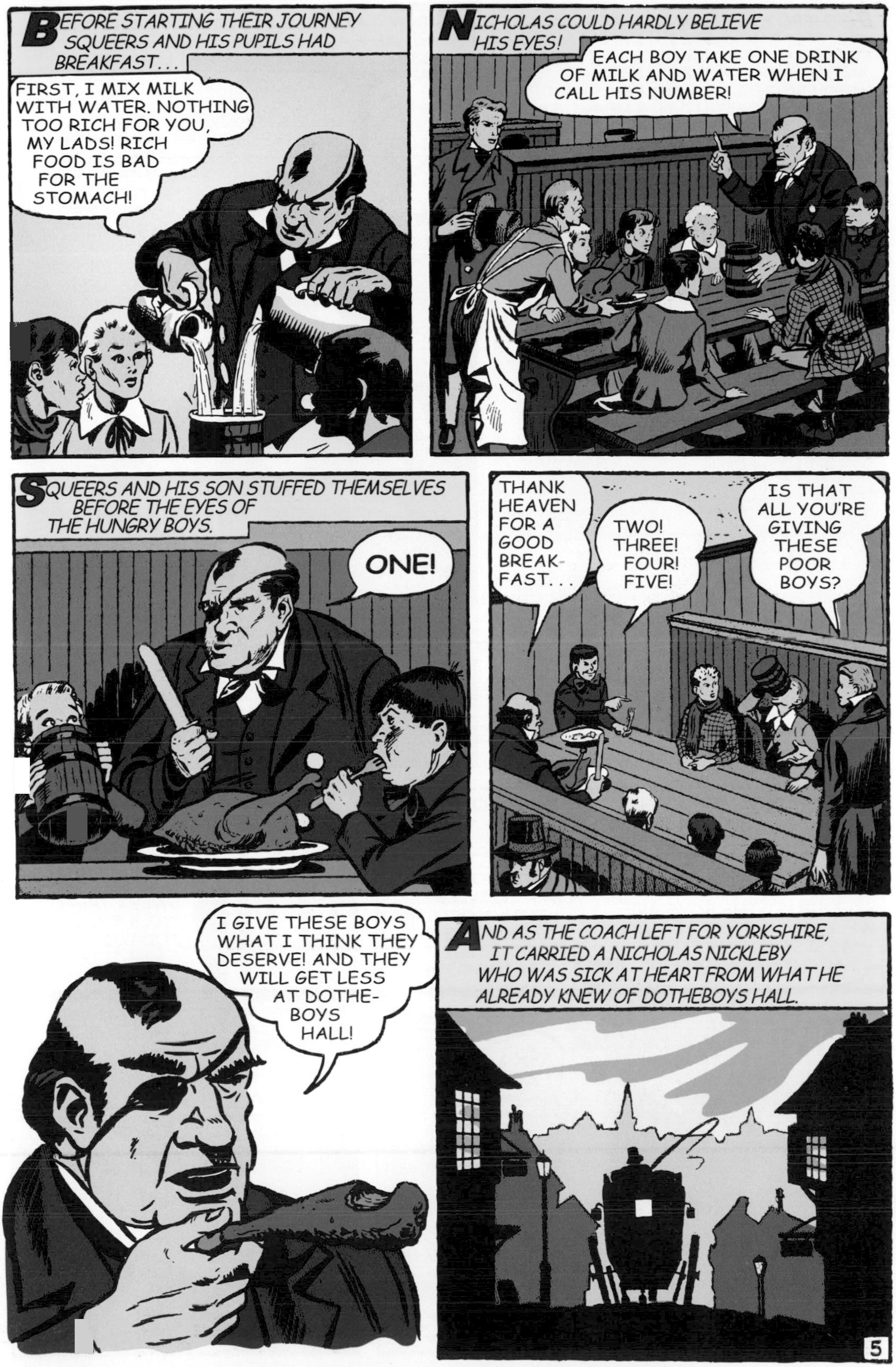
BEFORE STARTING THEIR JOURNEY SQUEERS AND HIS PUPILS HAD BREAKFAST...
FIRST, I MIX MILK WITH WATER. NOTHING TOO RICH FOR YOU, MY LADS! RICH FOOD IS BAD FOR THE STOMACH!
NICHOLAS COULD HARDLY BELIEVE HIS EYES!
EACH BOY TAKE ONE DRINK OF MILK AND WATER WHEN I CALL HIS NUMBER!
SQUEERS AND HIS SON STUFFED THEMSELVES BEFORE THE EYES OF THE HUNGRY BOYS.
ONE!
THANK HEAVEN FOR A GOOD BREAK-FAST...
TWO! THREE! FOUR! FIVE!
IS THAT ALL YOU'RE GIVING THESE POOR BOYS?
I GIVE THESE BOYS WHAT I THINK THEY DESERVE! AND THEY WILL GET LESS AT DOTHE-BOYS HALL!
AND AS THE COACH LEFT FOR YORKSHIRE, IT CARRIED A NICHOLAS NICKLEBY WHO WAS SICK AT HEART FROM WHAT HE ALREADY KNEW OF DOTHEBOYS HALL.
5

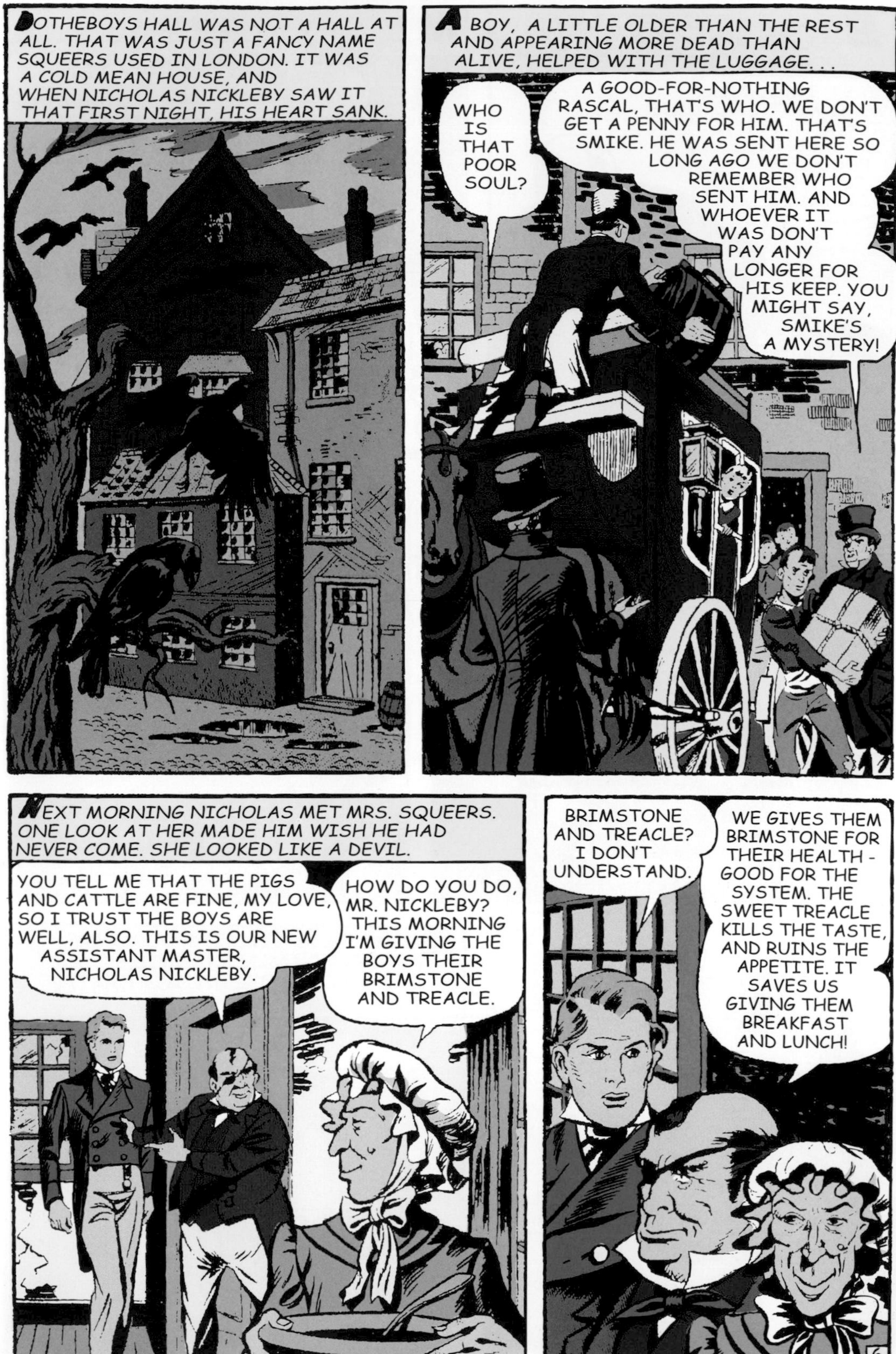
DOTHEBOYS HALL WAS NOT A HALL AT ALL. THAT WAS JUST A FANCY NAME SQUEERS USED IN LONDON. IT WAS A COLD MEAN HOUSE, AND WHEN NICHOLAS NICKLEBY SAW IT THAT FIRST NIGHT, HIS HEART SANK.
A BOY, A LITTLE OLDER THAN THE REST AND APPEARING MORE DEAD THAN ALIVE, HELPED WITH THE LUGGAGE. . .
WHO IS THAT POOR SOUL?
A GOOD-FOR-NOTHING RASCAL, THAT'S WHO. WE DON'T GET A PENNY FOR HIM. THAT'S SMIKE. HE WAS SENT HERE SO LONG AGO WE DON'T REMEMBER WHO SENT HIM. AND WHOEVER IT WAS DON'T PAY ANY LONGER FOR HIS KEEP. YOU MIGHT SAY, SMIKE'S A MYSTERY!
NEXT MORNING NICHOLAS MET MRS. SQUEERS. ONE LOOK AT HER MADE HIM WISH HE HAD NEVER COME. SHE LOOKED LIKE A DEVIL.
YOU TELL ME THAT THE PIGS AND CATTLE ARE FINE, MY LOVE, SO I TRUST THE BOYS ARE WELL, ALSO. THIS IS OUR NEW ASSISTANT MASTER, NICHOLAS NICKLEBY.
HOW DO YOU DO, MR. NICKLEBY? THIS MORNING I'M GIVING THE BOYS THEIR BRIMSTONE AND TREACLE.
BRIMSTONE AND TREACLE? I DON'T UNDERSTAND.
WE GIVES THEM BRIMSTONE FOR THEIR HEALTH - GOOD FOR THE SYSTEM. THE SWEET TREACLE KILLS THE TASTE, AND RUINS THE APPETITE. IT SAVES US GIVING THEM BREAKFAST AND LUNCH!
6

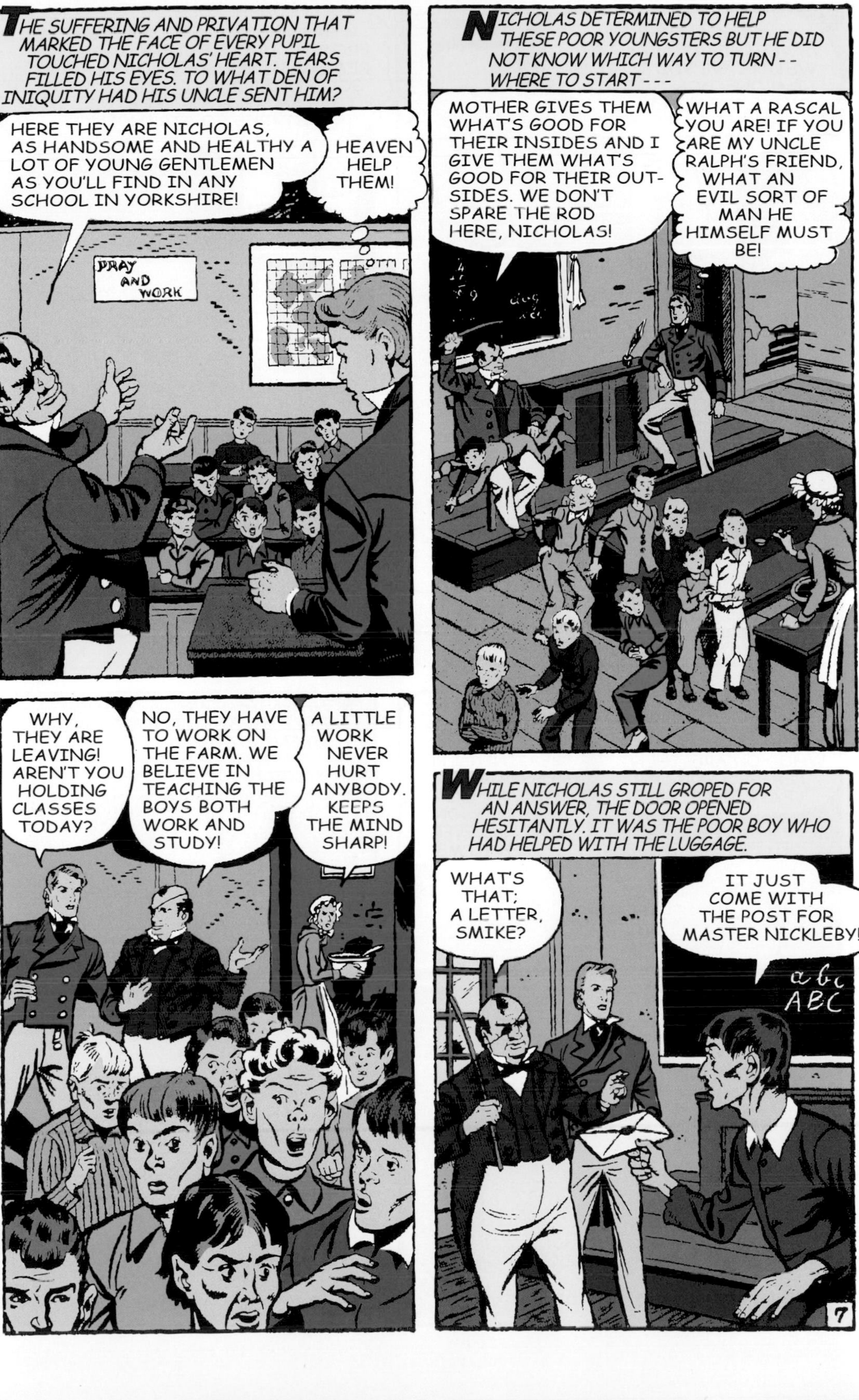
THE SUFFERING AND PRIVATION THAT MARKED THE FACE OF EVERY PUPIL TOUCHED NICHOLAS' HEART. TEARS FILLED HIS EYES. TO WHAT DEN OF INIQUITY HAD HIS UNCLE SENT HIM?
HERE THEY ARE NICHOLAS, AS HANDSOME AND HEALTHY A LOT OF YOUNG GENTLEMEN AS YOU'LL FIND IN ANY SCHOOL IN YORKSHIRE!
HEAVEN HELP THEM!
PRAY AND WORK
NICHOLAS DETERMINED TO HELP THESE POOR YOUNGSTERS BUT HE DID NOT KNOW WHICH WAY TO TURN - - WHERE TO START - - -
MOTHER GIVES THEM WHAT'S GOOD FOR THEIR INSIDES AND I GIVE THEM WHAT'S GOOD FOR THEIR OUT-SIDES. WE DON'T SPARE THE ROD HERE, NICHOLAS!
WHAT A RASCAL YOU ARE! IF YOU ARE MY UNCLE RALPH'S FRIEND, WHAT AN EVIL SORT OF MAN HE HIMSELF MUST BE!
WHY, THEY ARE LEAVING! AREN'T YOU HOLDING CLASSES TODAY?
NO, THEY HAVE TO WORK ON THE FARM. WE BELIEVE IN TEACHING THE BOYS BOTH WORK AND STUDY!
A LITTLE WORK NEVER HURT ANYBODY. KEEPS THE MIND SHARP!
WHILE NICHOLAS STILL GROPED FOR AN ANSWER, THE DOOR OPENED HESITANTLY. IT WAS THE POOR BOY WHO HAD HELPED WITH THE LUGGAGE.
WHAT'S THAT; A LETTER, SMIKE?
IT JUST COME WITH THE POST FOR MASTER NICKLEBY!
a b c
ABC
7

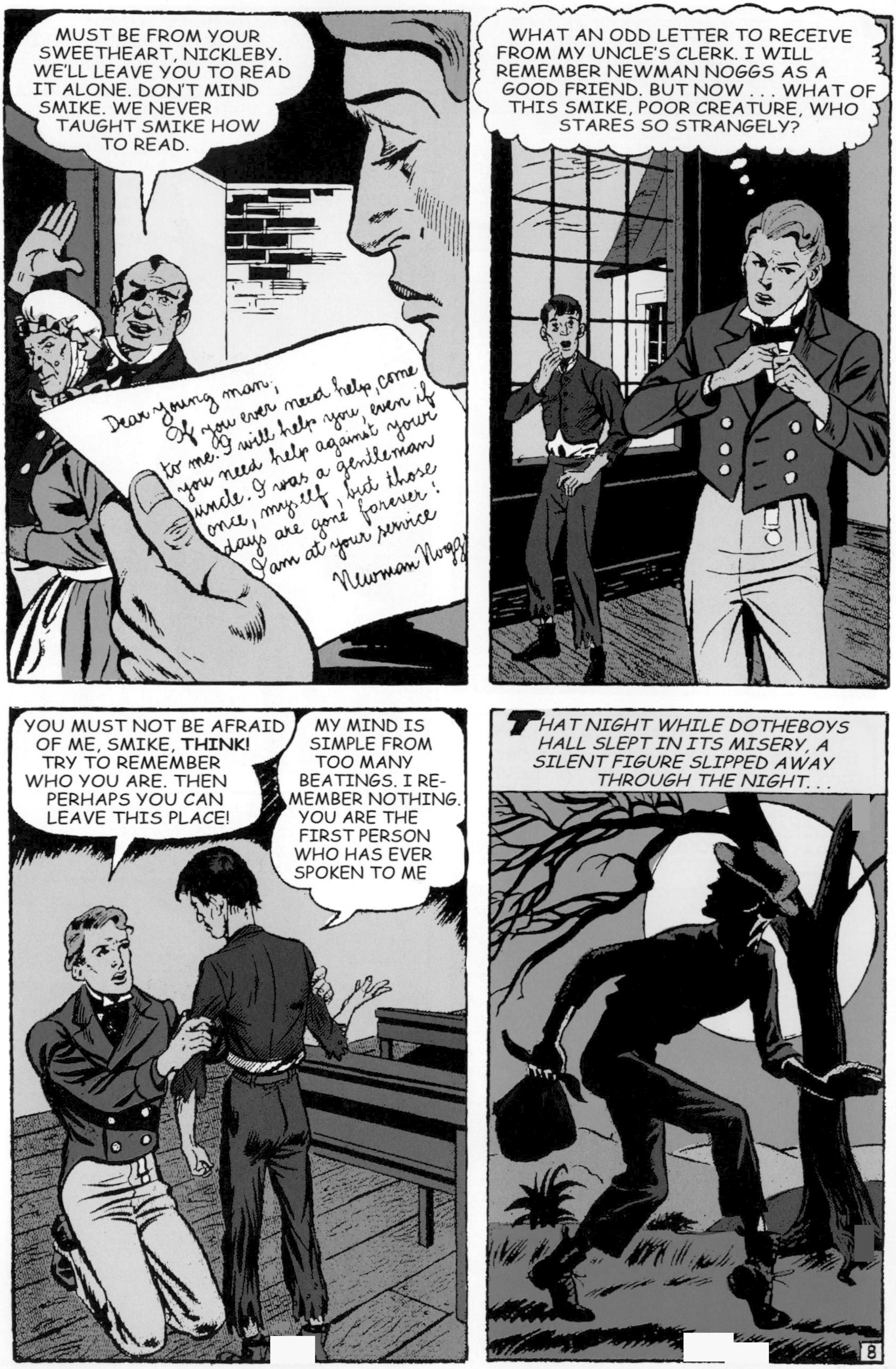
MUST BE FROM YOUR SWEETHEART, NICKLEBY. WE'LL LEAVE YOU TO READ IT ALONE. DON'T MIND SMIKE. WE NEVER TAUGHT SMIKE HOW TO READ.
Dear young man,
If you ever need help, come to me. I will help you, even if you need help against your uncle. I was a gentleman once, myself, but those days are gone forever!
I am at your service
Newman Noggs
WHAT AN ODD LETTER TO RECEIVE FROM MY UNCLE'S CLERK. I WILL REMEMBER NEWMAN NOGGS AS A GOOD FRIEND. BUT NOW . . . WHAT OF THIS SMIKE, POOR CREATURE, WHO STARES SO STRANGELY?
YOU MUST NOT BE AFRAID OF ME, SMIKE, THINK! TRY TO REMEMBER WHO YOU ARE. THEN PERHAPS YOU CAN LEAVE THIS PLACE!
MY MIND IS SIMPLE FROM TOO MANY BEATINGS. I REMEMBER NOTHING. YOU ARE THE FIRST PERSON WHO HAS EVER SPOKEN TO ME
THAT NIGHT WHILE DOTHEBOYS HALL SLEPT IN ITS MISERY, A SILENT FIGURE SLIPPED AWAY THROUGH THE NIGHT. . .
8

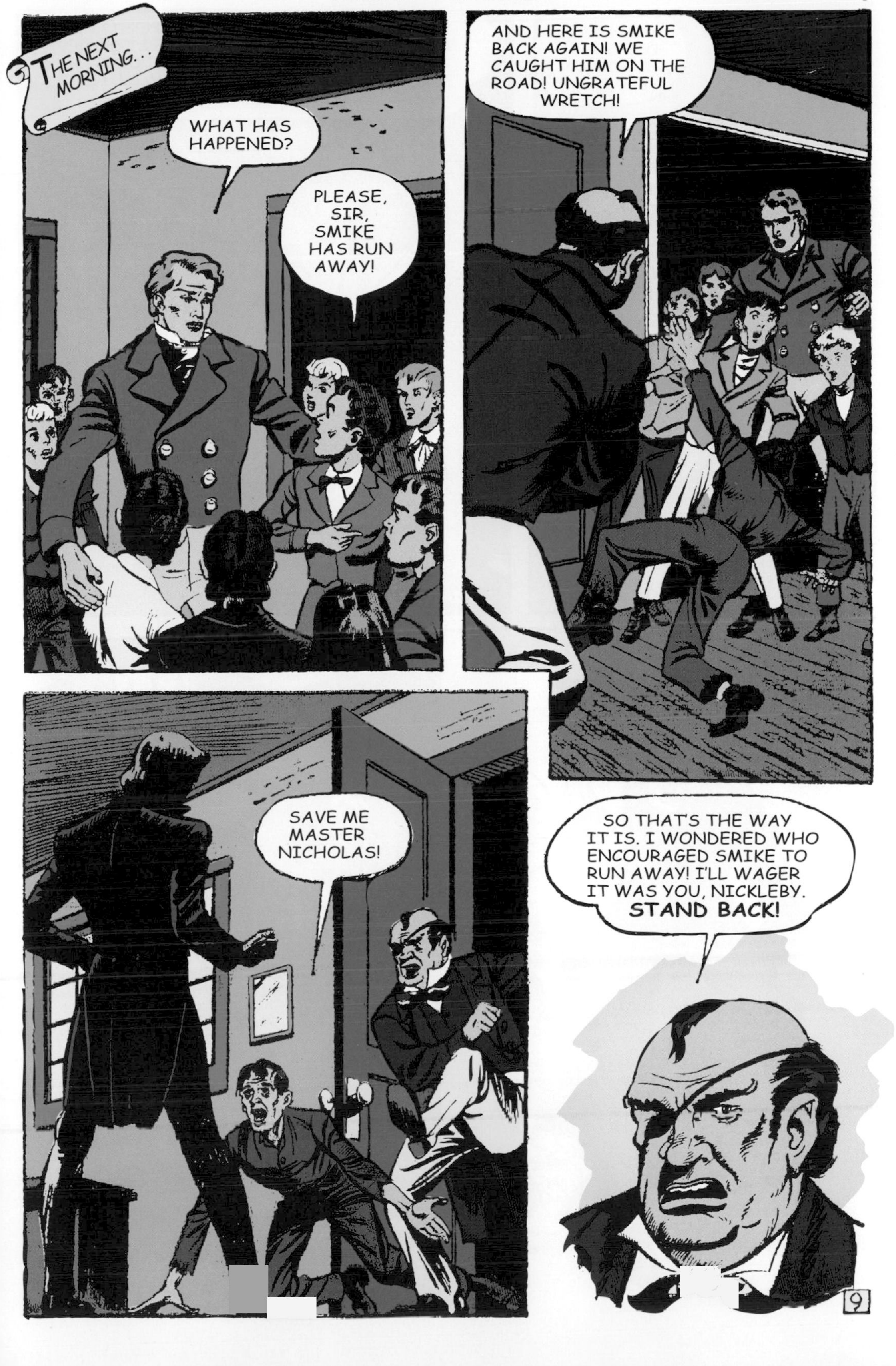
THE NEXT MORNING...
WHAT HAS HAPPENED?
PLEASE, SIR, SMIKE HAS RUN AWAY!
AND HERE IS SMIKE BACK AGAIN! WE CAUGHT HIM ON THE ROAD! UNGRATEFUL WRETCH!
SAVE ME MASTER NICHOLAS!
SO THAT'S THE WAY IT IS. I WONDERED WHO ENCOURAGED SMIKE TO RUN AWAY! I'LL WAGER IT WAS YOU, NICKLEBY. **STAND BACK!**
9

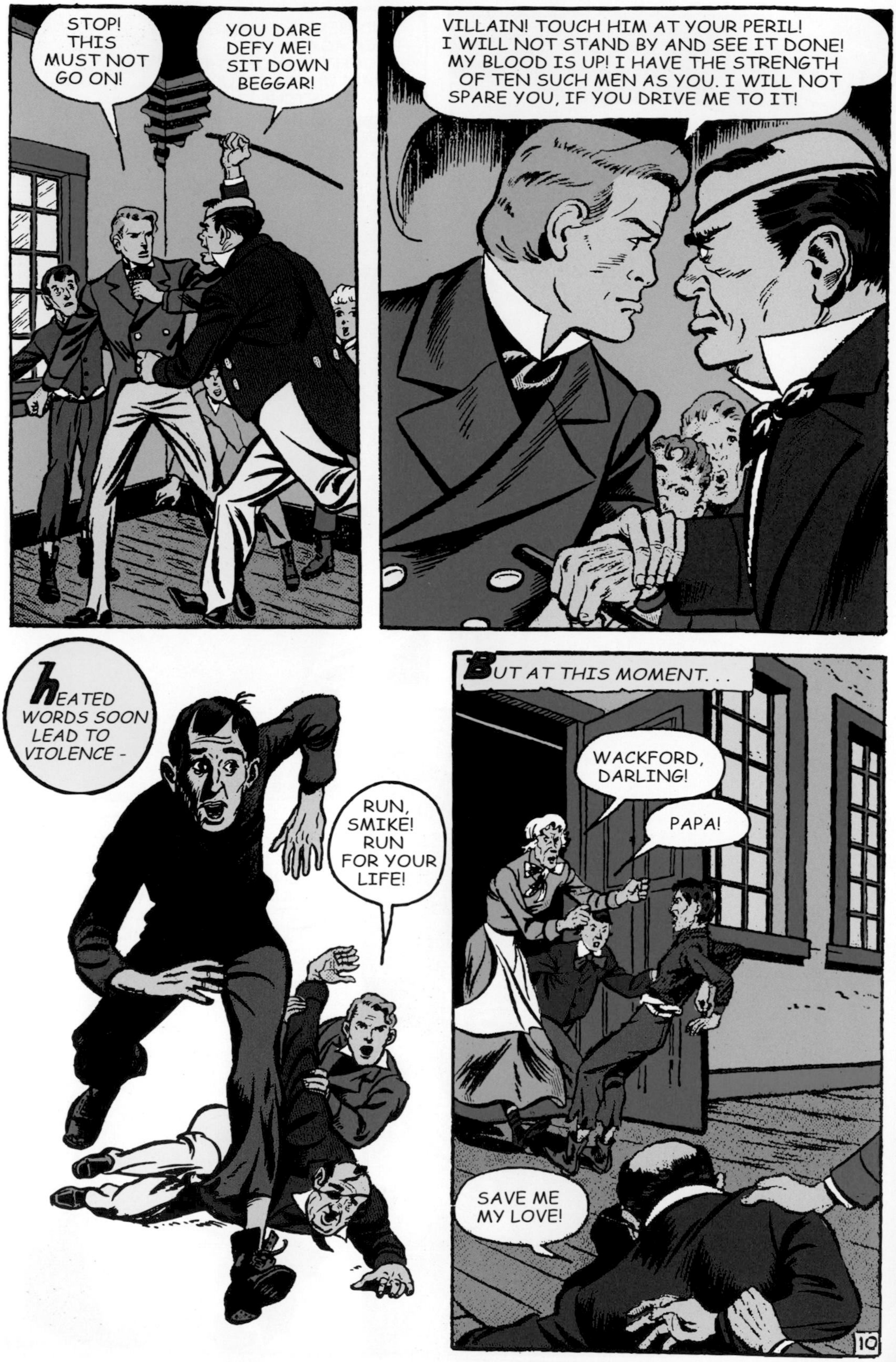
STOP! THIS MUST NOT GO ON!
YOU DARE DEFY ME! SIT DOWN BEGGAR!
VILLAIN! TOUCH HIM AT YOUR PERIL! I WILL NOT STAND BY AND SEE IT DONE! MY BLOOD IS UP! I HAVE THE STRENGTH OF TEN SUCH MEN AS YOU. I WILL NOT SPARE YOU, IF YOU DRIVE ME TO IT!
HEATED WORDS SOON LEAD TO VIOLENCE -
RUN, SMIKE! RUN FOR YOUR LIFE!
BUT AT THIS MOMENT. . .
WACKFORD, DARLING!
PAPA!
SAVE ME MY LOVE!
10

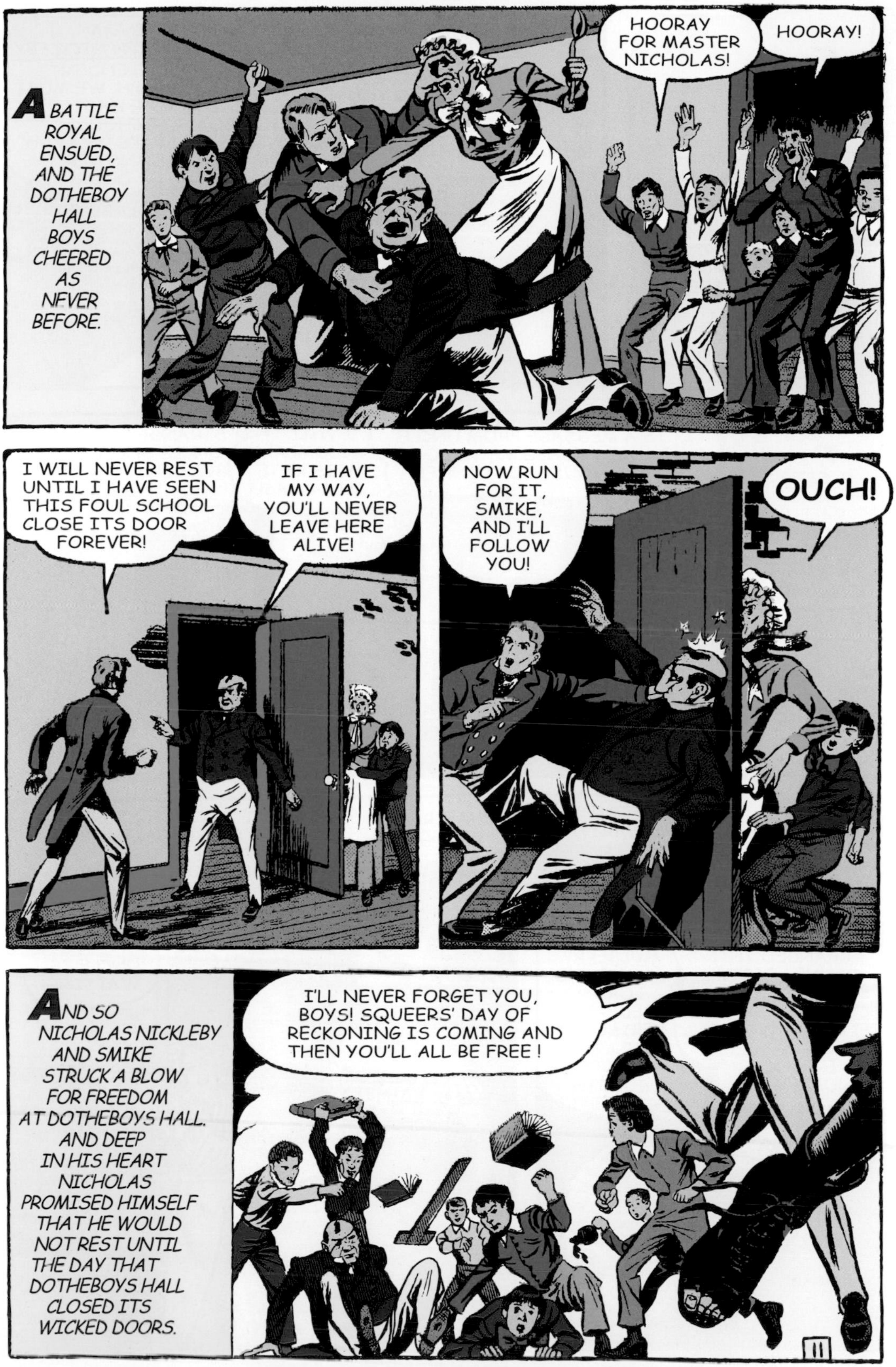
A BATTLE ROYAL ENSUED, AND THE DOTHEBOY HALL BOYS CHEERED AS NEVER BEFORE.
HOORAY FOR MASTER NICHOLAS!
HOORAY!
I WILL NEVER REST UNTIL I HAVE SEEN THIS FOUL SCHOOL CLOSE ITS DOOR FOREVER!
IF I HAVE MY WAY, YOU'LL NEVER LEAVE HERE ALIVE!
NOW RUN FOR IT, SMIKE, AND I'LL FOLLOW YOU!
OUCH!
AND SO NICHOLAS NICKLEBY AND SMIKE STRUCK A BLOW FOR FREEDOM AT DOTHEBOYS HALL. AND DEEP IN HIS HEART NICHOLAS PROMISED HIMSELF THAT HE WOULD NOT REST UNTIL THE DAY THAT DOTHEBOYS HALL CLOSED ITS WICKED DOORS.
I'LL NEVER FORGET YOU, BOYS! SQUEERS' DAY OF RECKONING IS COMING AND THEN YOU'LL ALL BE FREE !
11

LEAVING NICHOLAS AND HIS FRIEND SMIKE TO MAKE GOOD THEIR ESCAPE FROM DOTHEBOYS HALL, WE RETURN TO LONDON TO DISCOVER WHAT HAS HAPPENED TO NICHOLAS' MOTHER AND HIS SISTER, KATE...

MRS. NICKLEBY AND KATE HAD BEEN LODGED IN AN OLD DECREPIT MANSION OWNED BY UNCLE RALPH NICKLEBY.

SOMEONE'S KNOCKING AT THE DOOR, KATE. DO YOU THINK WE SHOULD ANSWER? THIS OLD HOUSE MAKES ME AFRAID.

SINCE WE ARE DEPENDENT UPON UNCLE RALPH, WE MUST LIVE WHERE HE HAS PLACED US. NICHOLAS WILL SOON TAKE US AWAY FROM HERE. I'LL ANSWER THE DOOR!

THE VISITOR WAS RALPH NICKLEBY'S CLERK, NEWMAN NOGGS.

IT IS A MESSAGE FROM UNCLE RALPH. HE WISHES ME TO COME TO HIS HOUSE FOR DINNER.

I WILL ACCOMPANY MISS KATE IN A COACH.

STRANGE THAT YOUR UNCLE SHOULD SUDDENLY BECOME SO KIND AND THOUGHTFUL.

WHILE KATE DRESSED FOR HER UNCLE'S DINNER PARTY...

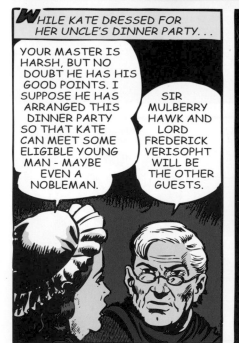

YOUR MASTER IS HARSH, BUT NO DOUBT HE HAS HIS GOOD POINTS. I SUPPOSE HE HAS ARRANGED THIS DINNER PARTY SO THAT KATE CAN MEET SOME ELIGIBLE YOUNG MAN - MAYBE EVEN A NOBLEMAN.

SIR MULBERRY HAWK AND LORD FREDERICK VERISOPHT WILL BE THE OTHER GUESTS.

I AM READY, MR. NOGGS.

IS KATE NOT THE SWEETEST AND MOST BEAUTIFUL GIRL IN LONDON? IF ONLY HER BROTHER, NICHOLAS COULD KNOW OF HER GOOD FORTUNE TONIGHT!

COME ALONG, MISS KATE. YOUR UNCLE IS WAITING!

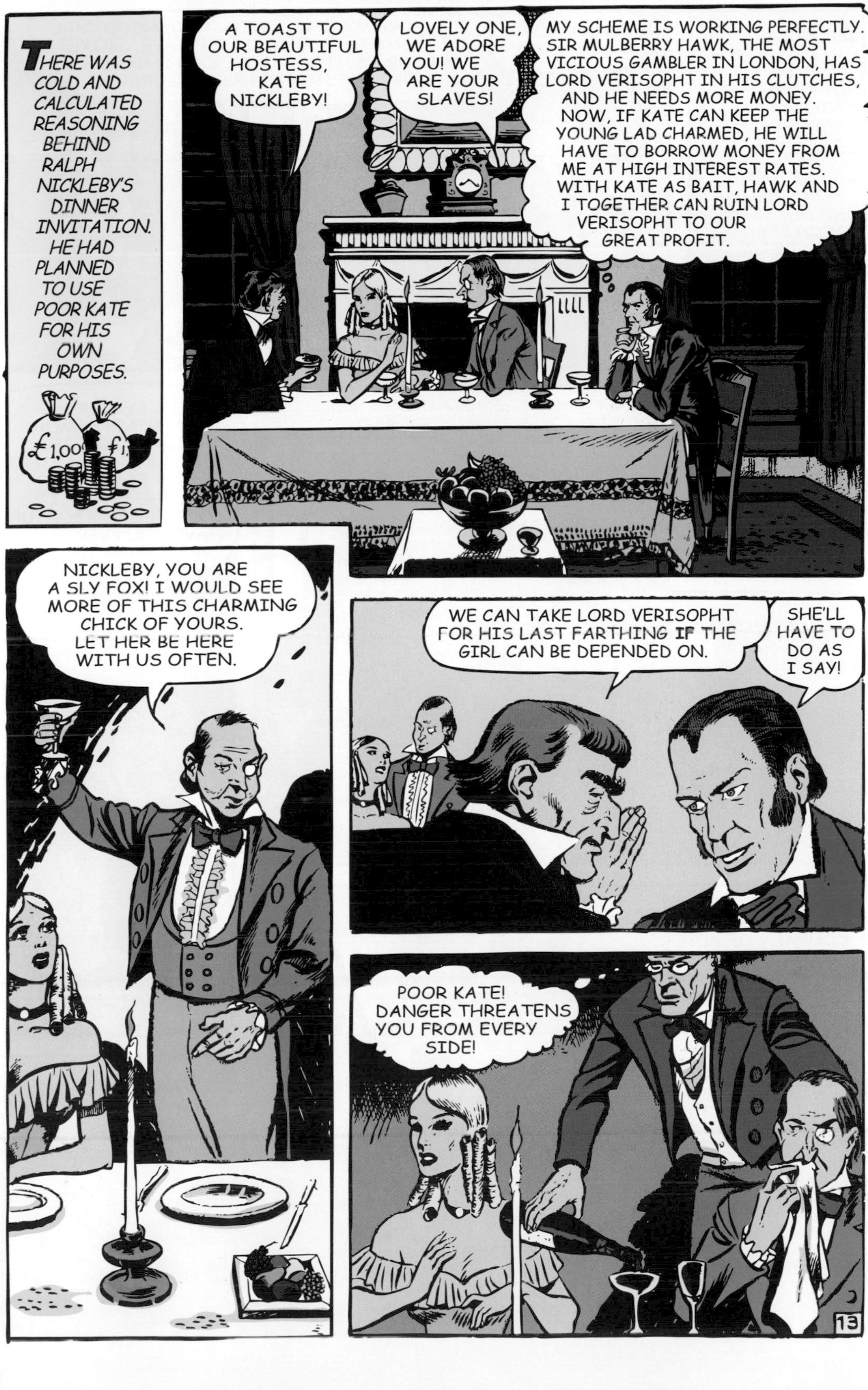
THERE WAS COLD AND CALCULATED REASONING BEHIND RALPH NICKLEBY'S DINNER INVITATION. HE HAD PLANNED TO USE POOR KATE FOR HIS OWN PURPOSES.
A TOAST TO OUR BEAUTIFUL HOSTESS, KATE NICKLEBY!
LOVELY ONE, WE ADORE YOU! WE ARE YOUR SLAVES!
MY SCHEME IS WORKING PERFECTLY. SIR MULBERRY HAWK, THE MOST VICIOUS GAMBLER IN LONDON, HAS LORD VERISOPHT IN HIS CLUTCHES, AND HE NEEDS MORE MONEY. NOW, IF KATE CAN KEEP THE YOUNG LAD CHARMED, HE WILL HAVE TO BORROW MONEY FROM ME AT HIGH INTEREST RATES. WITH KATE AS BAIT, HAWK AND I TOGETHER CAN RUIN LORD VERISOPHT TO OUR GREAT PROFIT.
NICKLEBY, YOU ARE A SLY FOX! I WOULD SEE MORE OF THIS CHARMING CHICK OF YOURS. LET HER BE HERE WITH US OFTEN.
WE CAN TAKE LORD VERISOPHT FOR HIS LAST FARTHING IF THE GIRL CAN BE DEPENDED ON.
SHE'LL HAVE TO DO AS I SAY!
POOR KATE! DANGER THREATENS YOU FROM EVERY SIDE!
13

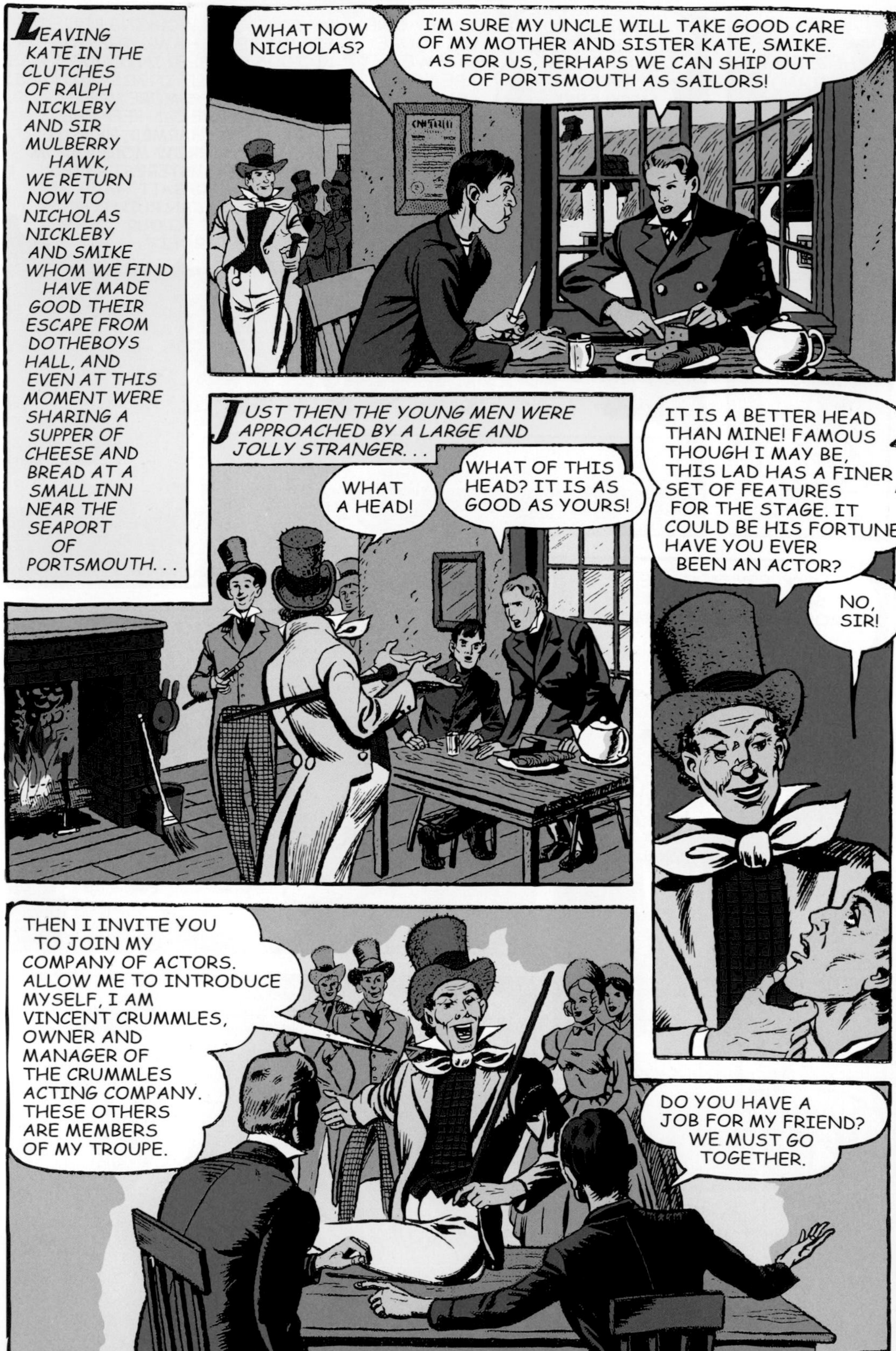
LEAVING KATE IN THE CLUTCHES OF RALPH NICKLEBY AND SIR MULBERRY HAWK, WE RETURN NOW TO NICHOLAS NICKLEBY AND SMIKE WHOM WE FIND HAVE MADE GOOD THEIR ESCAPE FROM DOTHEBOYS HALL, AND EVEN AT THIS MOMENT WERE SHARING A SUPPER OF CHEESE AND BREAD AT A SMALL INN NEAR THE SEAPORT OF PORTSMOUTH. . .
WHAT NOW NICHOLAS?
I'M SURE MY UNCLE WILL TAKE GOOD CARE OF MY MOTHER AND SISTER KATE, SMIKE. AS FOR US, PERHAPS WE CAN SHIP OUT OF PORTSMOUTH AS SAILORS!
JUST THEN THE YOUNG MEN WERE APPROACHED BY A LARGE AND JOLLY STRANGER. . .
WHAT A HEAD!
WHAT OF THIS HEAD? IT IS AS GOOD AS YOURS!
IT IS A BETTER HEAD THAN MINE! FAMOUS THOUGH I MAY BE, THIS LAD HAS A FINER SET OF FEATURES FOR THE STAGE. IT COULD BE HIS FORTUNE. HAVE YOU EVER BEEN AN ACTOR?
NO, SIR!
THEN I INVITE YOU TO JOIN MY COMPANY OF ACTORS. ALLOW ME TO INTRODUCE MYSELF, I AM VINCENT CRUMMLES, OWNER AND MANAGER OF THE CRUMMLES ACTING COMPANY. THESE OTHERS ARE MEMBERS OF MY TROUPE.
DO YOU HAVE A JOB FOR MY FRIEND? WE MUST GO TOGETHER.
14

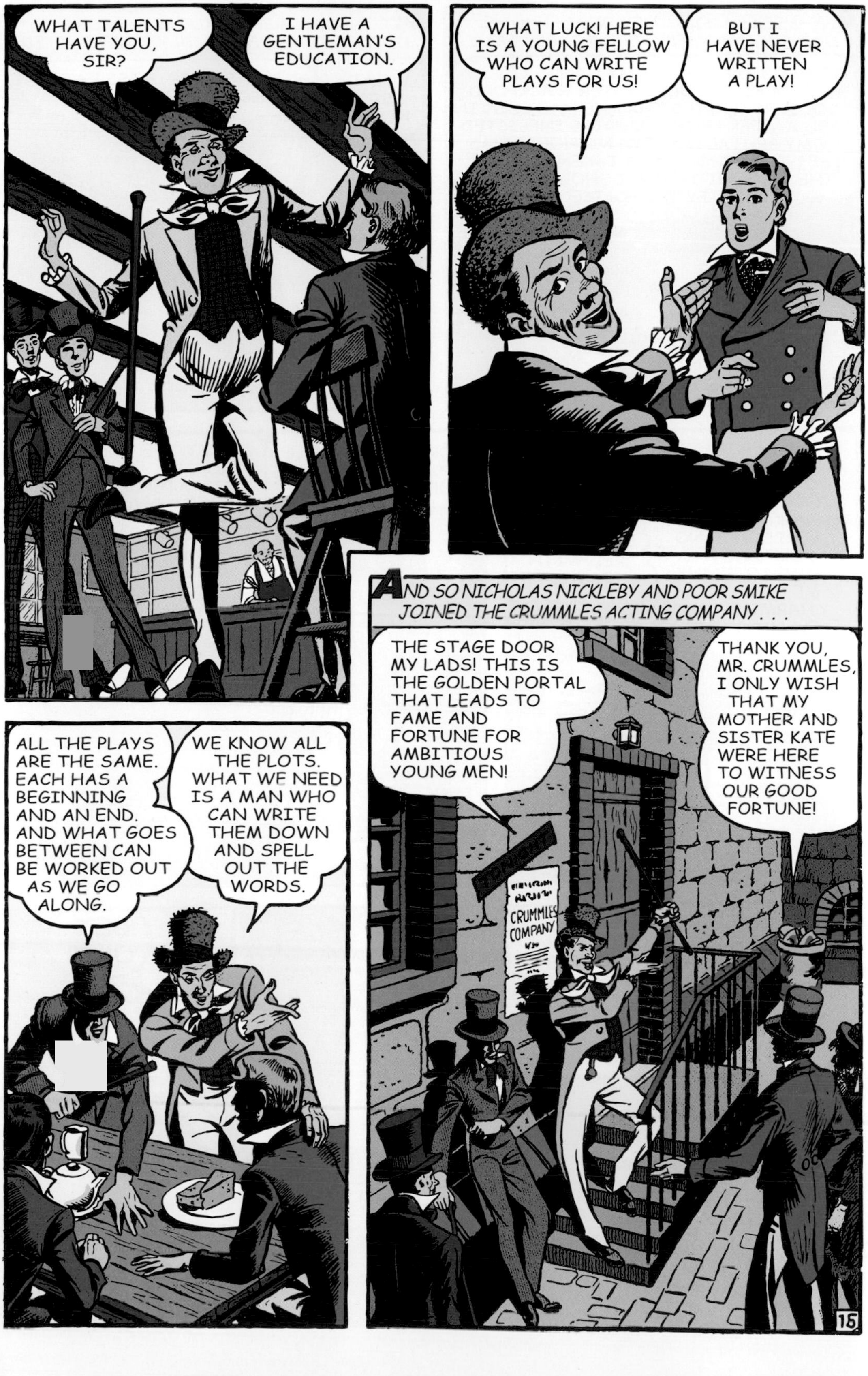
WHAT TALENTS HAVE YOU, SIR?
I HAVE A GENTLEMAN'S EDUCATION.
WHAT LUCK! HERE IS A YOUNG FELLOW WHO CAN WRITE PLAYS FOR US!
BUT I HAVE NEVER WRITTEN A PLAY!
ALL THE PLAYS ARE THE SAME. EACH HAS A BEGINNING AND AN END. AND WHAT GOES BETWEEN CAN BE WORKED OUT AS WE GO ALONG.
WE KNOW ALL THE PLOTS. WHAT WE NEED IS A MAN WHO CAN WRITE THEM DOWN AND SPELL OUT THE WORDS.
AND SO NICHOLAS NICKLEBY AND POOR SMIKE JOINED THE CRUMMLES ACTING COMPANY . . .
THE STAGE DOOR MY LADS! THIS IS THE GOLDEN PORTAL THAT LEADS TO FAME AND FORTUNE FOR AMBITIOUS YOUNG MEN!
THANK YOU, MR. CRUMMLES, I ONLY WISH THAT MY MOTHER AND SISTER KATE WERE HERE TO WITNESS OUR GOOD FORTUNE!
CRUMMLES COMPANY
15

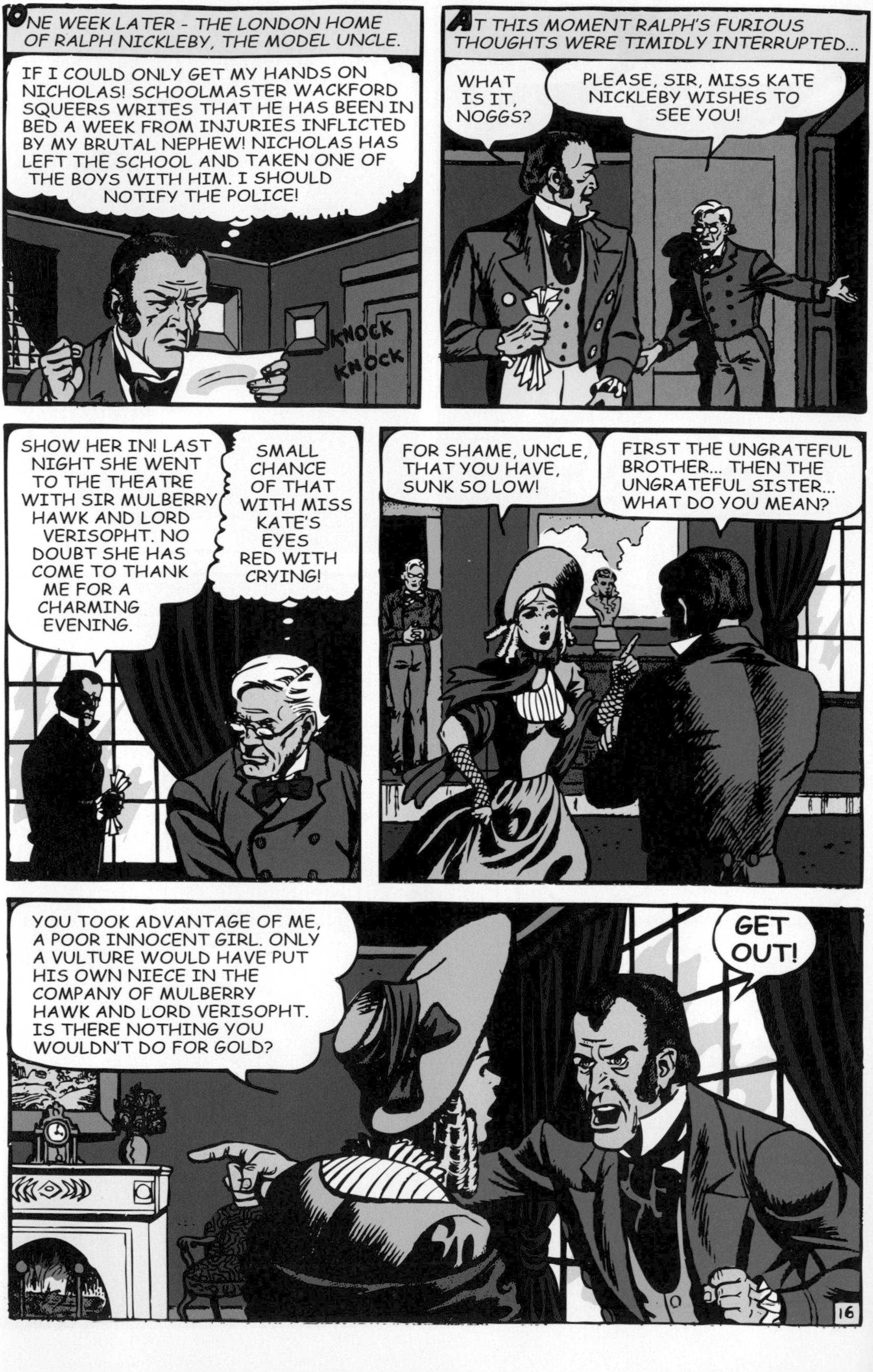
ONE WEEK LATER - THE LONDON HOME OF RALPH NICKLEBY, THE MODEL UNCLE.
IF I COULD ONLY GET MY HANDS ON NICHOLAS! SCHOOLMASTER WACKFORD SQUEERS WRITES THAT HE HAS BEEN IN BED A WEEK FROM INJURIES INFLICTED BY MY BRUTAL NEPHEW! NICHOLAS HAS LEFT THE SCHOOL AND TAKEN ONE OF THE BOYS WITH HIM. I SHOULD NOTIFY THE POLICE!
KNOCK KNOCK
AT THIS MOMENT RALPH'S FURIOUS THOUGHTS WERE TIMIDLY INTERRUPTED...
WHAT IS IT, NOGGS?
PLEASE, SIR, MISS KATE NICKLEBY WISHES TO SEE YOU!
SHOW HER IN! LAST NIGHT SHE WENT TO THE THEATRE WITH SIR MULBERRY HAWK AND LORD VERISOPHT. NO DOUBT SHE HAS COME TO THANK ME FOR A CHARMING EVENING.
SMALL CHANCE OF THAT WITH MISS KATE'S EYES RED WITH CRYING!
FOR SHAME, UNCLE, THAT YOU HAVE, SUNK SO LOW!
FIRST THE UNGRATEFUL BROTHER... THEN THE UNGRATEFUL SISTER... WHAT DO YOU MEAN?
YOU TOOK ADVANTAGE OF ME, A POOR INNOCENT GIRL. ONLY A VULTURE WOULD HAVE PUT HIS OWN NIECE IN THE COMPANY OF MULBERRY HAWK AND LORD VERISOPHT. IS THERE NOTHING YOU WOULDN'T DO FOR GOLD?
GET OUT!
16

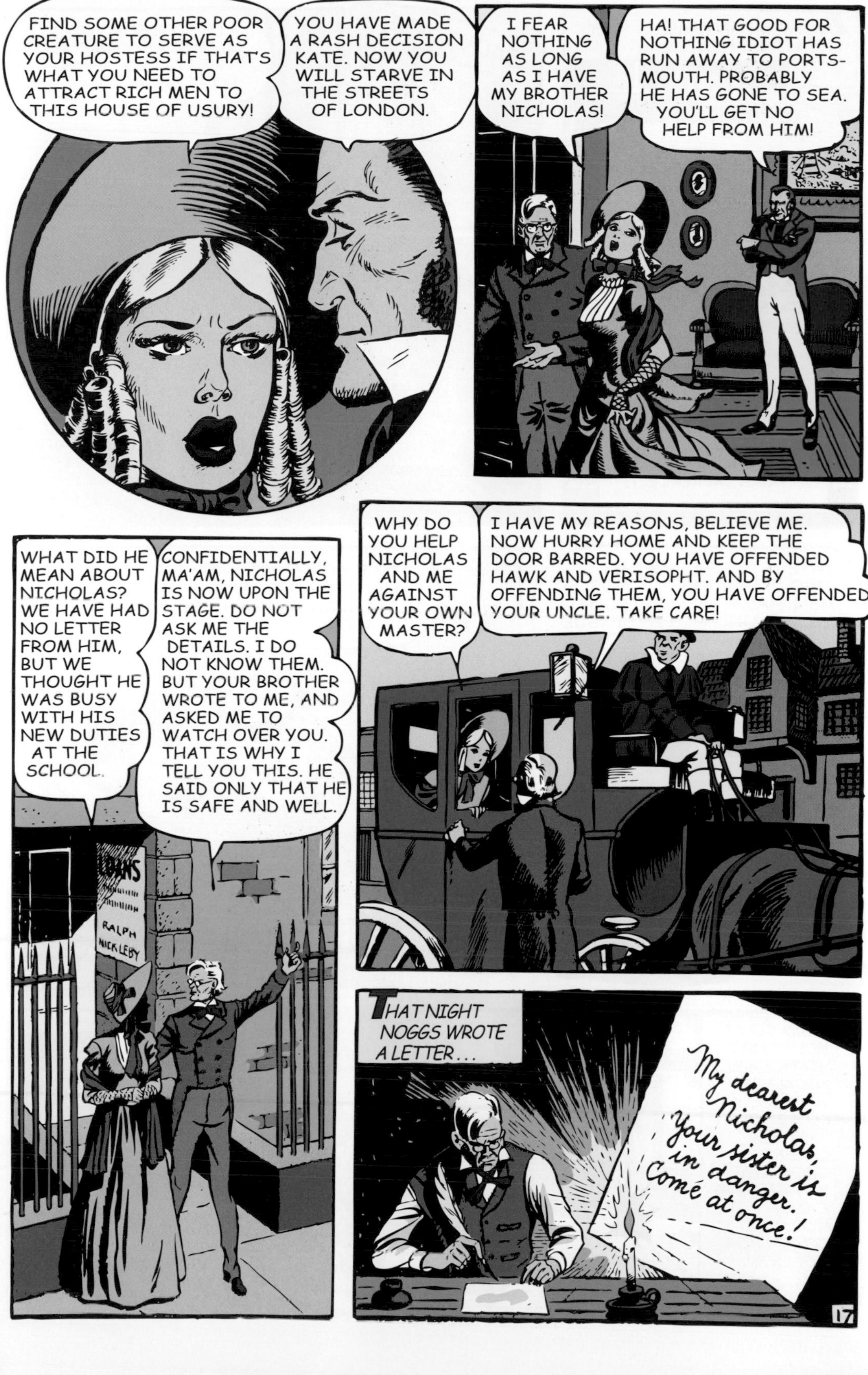
FIND SOME OTHER POOR CREATURE TO SERVE AS YOUR HOSTESS IF THAT'S WHAT YOU NEED TO ATTRACT RICH MEN TO THIS HOUSE OF USURY!
YOU HAVE MADE A RASH DECISION KATE. NOW YOU WILL STARVE IN THE STREETS OF LONDON.
I FEAR NOTHING AS LONG AS I HAVE MY BROTHER NICHOLAS!
HA! THAT GOOD FOR NOTHING IDIOT HAS RUN AWAY TO PORTS-MOUTH. PROBABLY HE HAS GONE TO SEA. YOU'LL GET NO HELP FROM HIM!
WHAT DID HE MEAN ABOUT NICHOLAS? WE HAVE HAD NO LETTER FROM HIM, BUT WE THOUGHT HE WAS BUSY WITH HIS NEW DUTIES AT THE SCHOOL.
CONFIDENTIALLY, MA'AM, NICHOLAS IS NOW UPON THE STAGE. DO NOT ASK ME THE DETAILS. I DO NOT KNOW THEM. BUT YOUR BROTHER WROTE TO ME, AND ASKED ME TO WATCH OVER YOU. THAT IS WHY I TELL YOU THIS. HE SAID ONLY THAT HE IS SAFE AND WELL.
LOANS
RALPH NICKLEBY
WHY DO YOU HELP NICHOLAS AND ME AGAINST YOUR OWN MASTER?
I HAVE MY REASONS, BELIEVE ME. NOW HURRY HOME AND KEEP THE DOOR BARRED. YOU HAVE OFFENDED HAWK AND VERISOPHT. AND BY OFFENDING THEM, YOU HAVE OFFENDED YOUR UNCLE. TAKE CARE!
THAT NIGHT NOGGS WROTE A LETTER...
My dearest Nicholas, Your sister is in danger. Come at once!
17

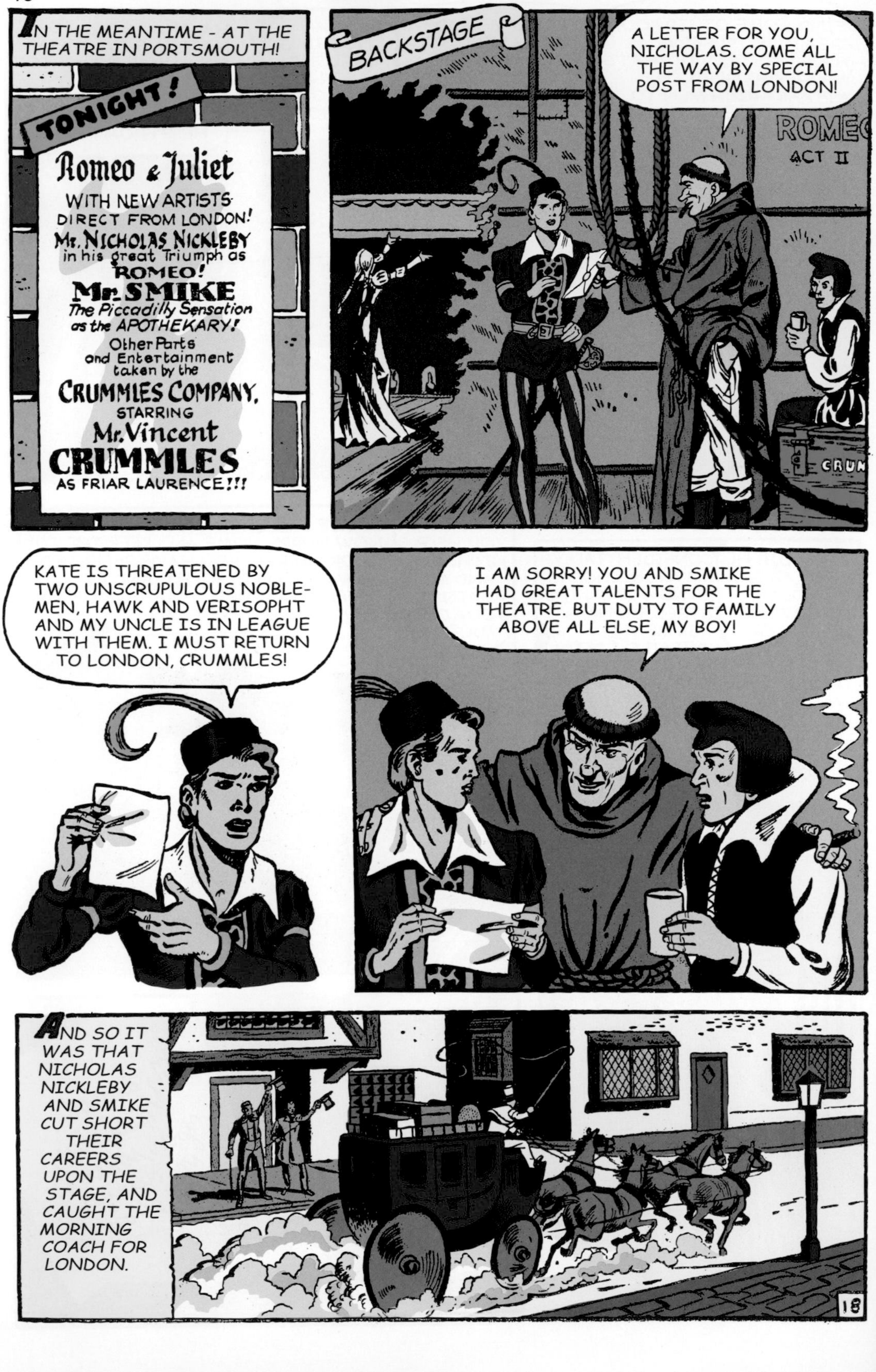
IN THE MEANTIME - AT THE THEATRE IN PORTSMOUTH!
TONIGHT!
Romeo & Juliet
WITH NEW ARTISTS DIRECT FROM LONDON!
Mr. NICHOLAS NICKLEBY in his great Triumph as ROMEO!
Mr. SMIKE The Piccadilly Sensation as the APOTHEKARY!
Other Parts and Entertainment taken by the
CRUMMLES COMPANY. STARRING
Mr. Vincent CRUMMLES AS FRIAR LAURENCE!!!
BACKSTAGE
A LETTER FOR YOU, NICHOLAS. COME ALL THE WAY BY SPECIAL POST FROM LONDON!
ROMEO
ACT II
KATE IS THREATENED BY TWO UNSCRUPULOUS NOBLE-MEN, HAWK AND VERISOPHT AND MY UNCLE IS IN LEAGUE WITH THEM. I MUST RETURN TO LONDON, CRUMMLES!
I AM SORRY! YOU AND SMIKE HAD GREAT TALENTS FOR THE THEATRE. BUT DUTY TO FAMILY ABOVE ALL ELSE, MY BOY!
AND SO IT WAS THAT NICHOLAS NICKLEBY AND SMIKE CUT SHORT THEIR CAREERS UPON THE STAGE, AND CAUGHT THE MORNING COACH FOR LONDON.
18

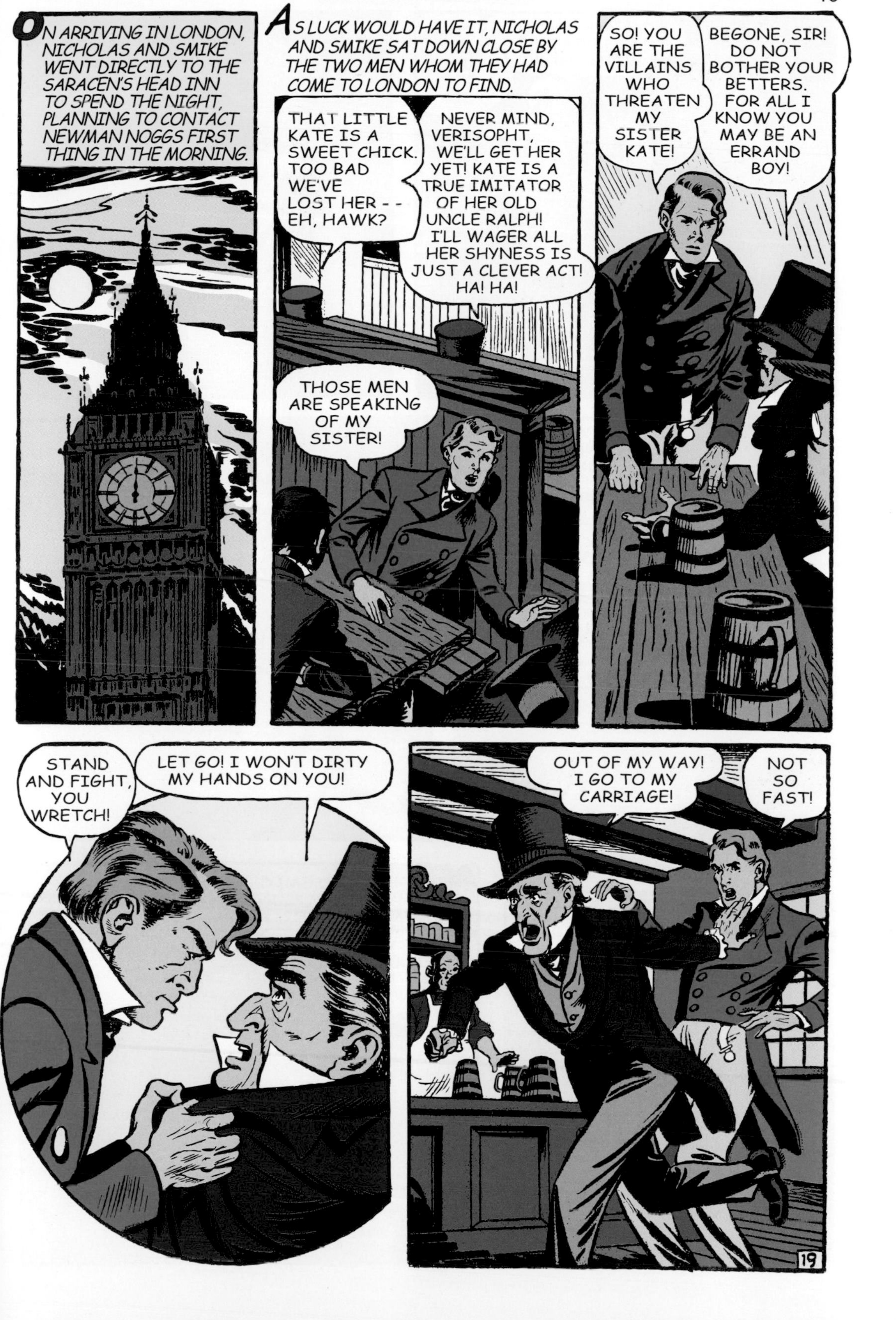
ON ARRIVING IN LONDON, NICHOLAS AND SMIKE WENT DIRECTLY TO THE SARACEN'S HEAD INN TO SPEND THE NIGHT, PLANNING TO CONTACT NEWMAN NOGGS FIRST THING IN THE MORNING.
AS LUCK WOULD HAVE IT, NICHOLAS AND SMIKE SAT DOWN CLOSE BY THE TWO MEN WHOM THEY HAD COME TO LONDON TO FIND.
THAT LITTLE KATE IS A SWEET CHICK. TOO BAD WE'VE LOST HER - - EH, HAWK?
NEVER MIND, VERISOPHT, WE'LL GET HER YET! KATE IS A TRUE IMITATOR OF HER OLD UNCLE RALPH! I'LL WAGER ALL HER SHYNESS IS JUST A CLEVER ACT! HA! HA!
THOSE MEN ARE SPEAKING OF MY SISTER!
SO! YOU ARE THE VILLAINS WHO THREATEN MY SISTER KATE!
BEGONE, SIR! DO NOT BOTHER YOUR BETTERS. FOR ALL I KNOW YOU MAY BE AN ERRAND BOY!
STAND AND FIGHT, YOU WRETCH!
LET GO! I WON'T DIRTY MY HANDS ON YOU!
OUT OF MY WAY! I GO TO MY CARRIAGE!
NOT SO FAST!
19

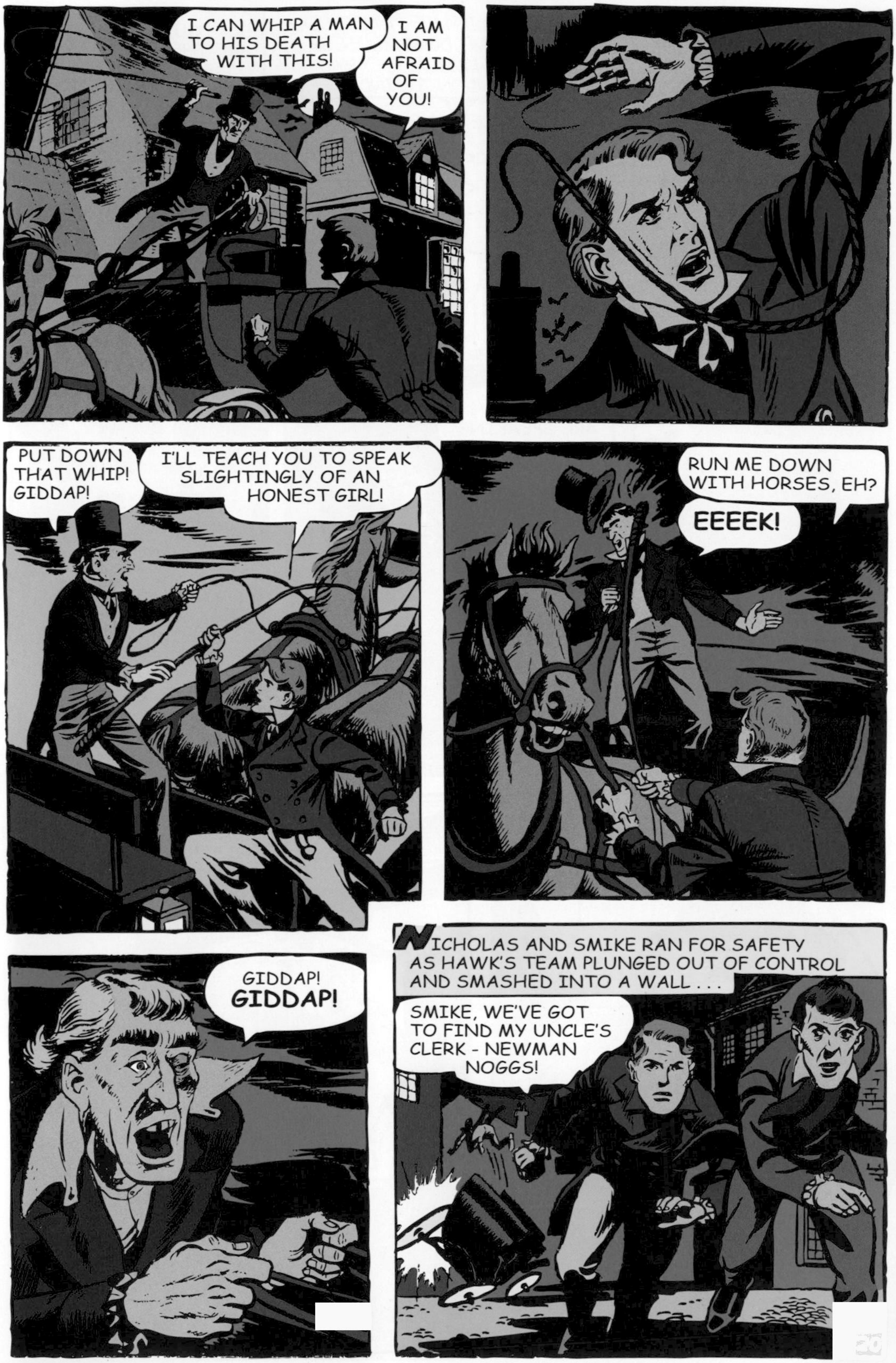
I CAN WHIP A MAN TO HIS DEATH WITH THIS!
I AM NOT AFRAID OF YOU!
PUT DOWN THAT WHIP! GIDDAP!
I'LL TEACH YOU TO SPEAK SLIGHTINGLY OF AN HONEST GIRL!
RUN ME DOWN WITH HORSES, EH?
EEEEK!
GIDDAP! GIDDAP!
NICHOLAS AND SMIKE RAN FOR SAFETY AS HAWK'S TEAM PLUNGED OUT OF CONTROL AND SMASHED INTO A WALL . . .
SMIKE, WE'VE GOT TO FIND MY UNCLE'S CLERK - NEWMAN NOGGS!

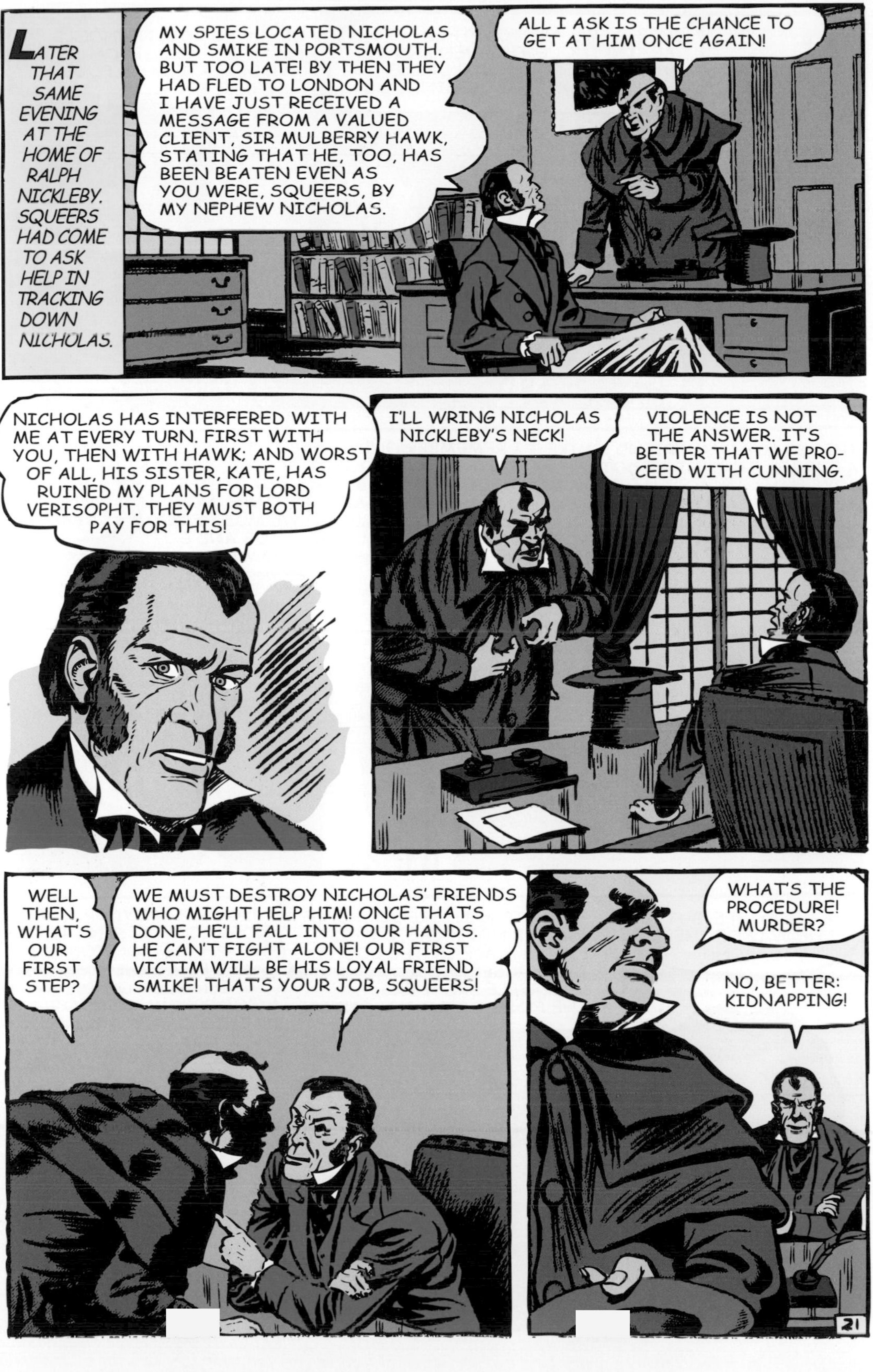
LATER THAT SAME EVENING AT THE HOME OF RALPH NICKLEBY. SQUEERS HAD COME TO ASK HELP IN TRACKING DOWN NICHOLAS.
MY SPIES LOCATED NICHOLAS AND SMIKE IN PORTSMOUTH. BUT TOO LATE! BY THEN THEY HAD FLED TO LONDON AND I HAVE JUST RECEIVED A MESSAGE FROM A VALUED CLIENT, SIR MULBERRY HAWK, STATING THAT HE, TOO, HAS BEEN BEATEN EVEN AS YOU WERE, SQUEERS, BY MY NEPHEW NICHOLAS.
ALL I ASK IS THE CHANCE TO GET AT HIM ONCE AGAIN!
NICHOLAS HAS INTERFERED WITH ME AT EVERY TURN. FIRST WITH YOU, THEN WITH HAWK; AND WORST OF ALL, HIS SISTER, KATE, HAS RUINED MY PLANS FOR LORD VERISOPHT. THEY MUST BOTH PAY FOR THIS!
I'LL WRING NICHOLAS NICKLEBY'S NECK!
VIOLENCE IS NOT THE ANSWER. IT'S BETTER THAT WE PRO-CEED WITH CUNNING.
WELL THEN, WHAT'S OUR FIRST STEP?
WE MUST DESTROY NICHOLAS' FRIENDS WHO MIGHT HELP HIM! ONCE THAT'S DONE, HE'LL FALL INTO OUR HANDS. HE CAN'T FIGHT ALONE! OUR FIRST VICTIM WILL BE HIS LOYAL FRIEND, SMIKE! THAT'S YOUR JOB, SQUEERS!
WHAT'S THE PROCEDURE! MURDER?
NO, BETTER: KIDNAPPING!
21

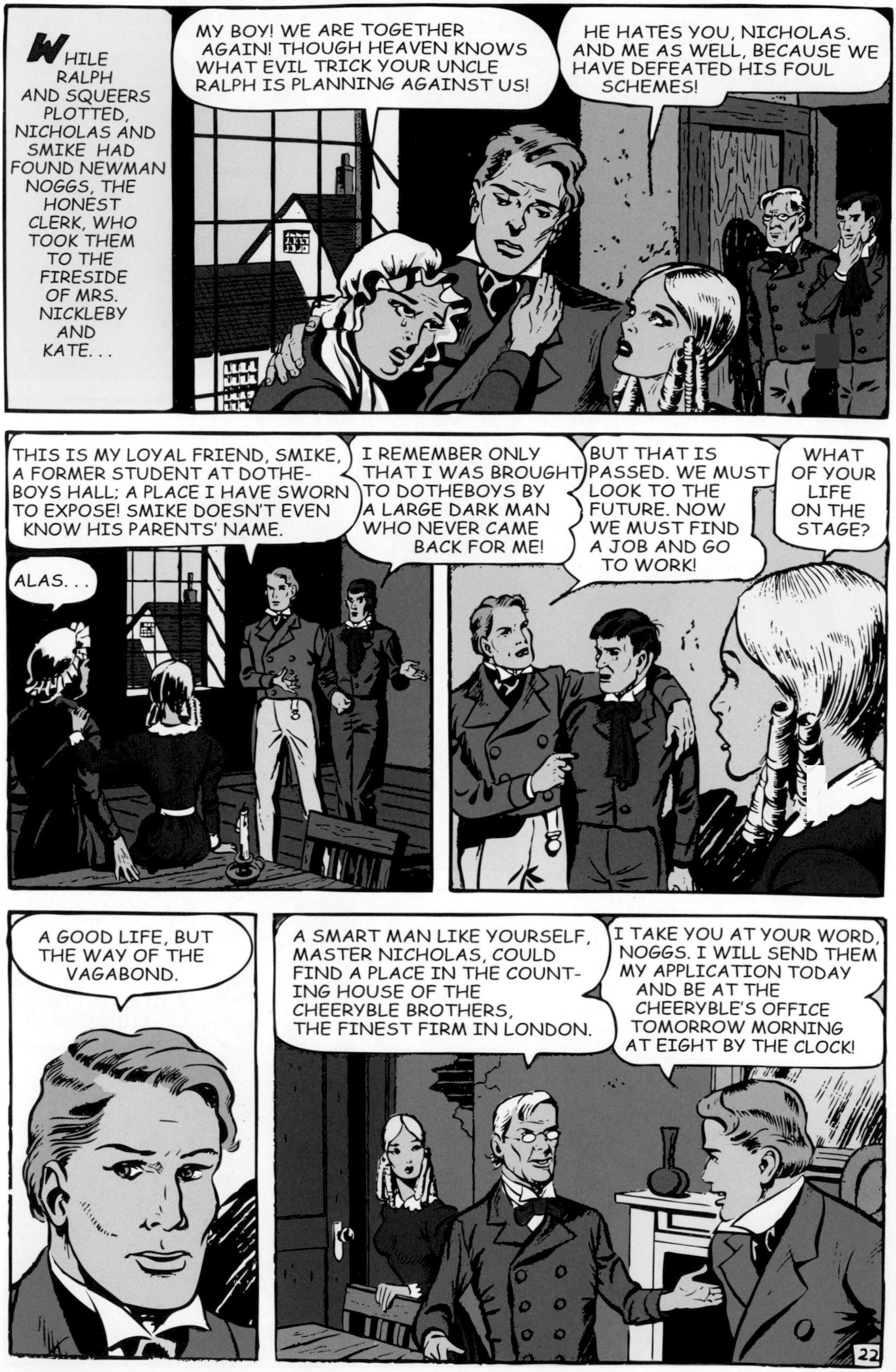
WHILE RALPH AND SQUEERS PLOTTED, NICHOLAS AND SMIKE HAD FOUND NEWMAN NOGGS, THE HONEST CLERK, WHO TOOK THEM TO THE FIRESIDE OF MRS. NICKLEBY AND KATE. . .
MY BOY! WE ARE TOGETHER AGAIN! THOUGH HEAVEN KNOWS WHAT EVIL TRICK YOUR UNCLE RALPH IS PLANNING AGAINST US!
HE HATES YOU, NICHOLAS. AND ME AS WELL, BECAUSE WE HAVE DEFEATED HIS FOUL SCHEMES!
THIS IS MY LOYAL FRIEND, SMIKE, A FORMER STUDENT AT DOTHE-BOYS HALL; A PLACE I HAVE SWORN TO EXPOSE! SMIKE DOESN'T EVEN KNOW HIS PARENTS' NAME.
ALAS. . .
I REMEMBER ONLY THAT I WAS BROUGHT TO DOTHEBOYS BY A LARGE DARK MAN WHO NEVER CAME BACK FOR ME!
BUT THAT IS PASSED. WE MUST LOOK TO THE FUTURE. NOW WE MUST FIND A JOB AND GO TO WORK!
WHAT OF YOUR LIFE ON THE STAGE?
A GOOD LIFE, BUT THE WAY OF THE VAGABOND.
A SMART MAN LIKE YOURSELF, MASTER NICHOLAS, COULD FIND A PLACE IN THE COUNT-ING HOUSE OF THE CHEERYBLE BROTHERS, THE FINEST FIRM IN LONDON.
I TAKE YOU AT YOUR WORD, NOGGS. I WILL SEND THEM MY APPLICATION TODAY AND BE AT THE CHEERYBLE'S OFFICE TOMORROW MORNING AT EIGHT BY THE CLOCK!
22

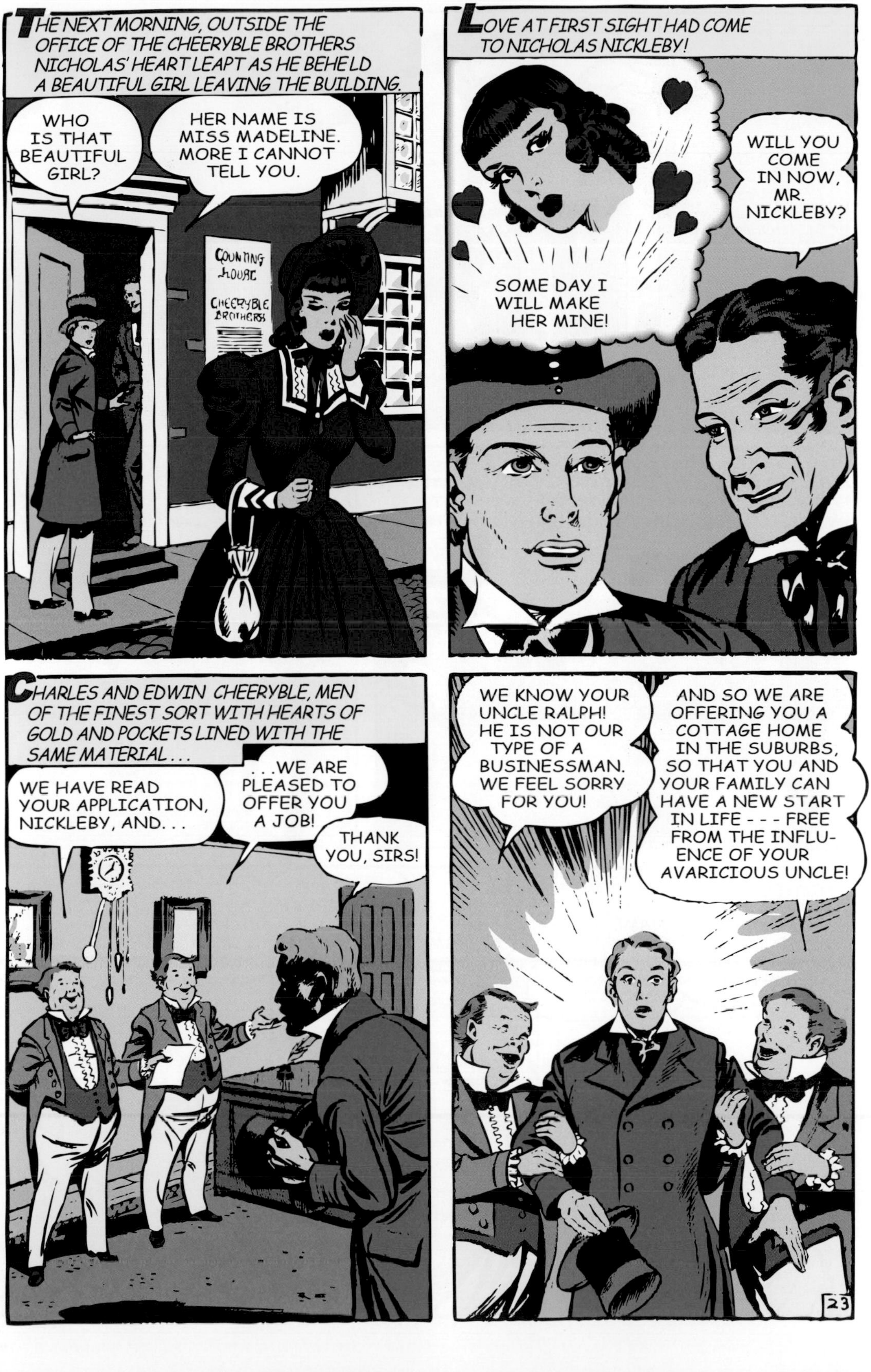
THE NEXT MORNING, OUTSIDE THE OFFICE OF THE CHEERYBLE BROTHERS NICHOLAS' HEART LEAPT AS HE BEHELD A BEAUTIFUL GIRL LEAVING THE BUILDING.
WHO IS THAT BEAUTIFUL GIRL?
HER NAME IS MISS MADELINE. MORE I CANNOT TELL YOU.
COUNTING HOUSE
CHEERYBLE BROTHERS
LOVE AT FIRST SIGHT HAD COME TO NICHOLAS NICKLEBY!
SOME DAY I WILL MAKE HER MINE!
WILL YOU COME IN NOW, MR. NICKLEBY?
CHARLES AND EDWIN CHEERYBLE, MEN OF THE FINEST SORT WITH HEARTS OF GOLD AND POCKETS LINED WITH THE SAME MATERIAL . . .
WE HAVE READ YOUR APPLICATION, NICKLEBY, AND. . .
. . .WE ARE PLEASED TO OFFER YOU A JOB!
THANK YOU, SIRS!
WE KNOW YOUR UNCLE RALPH! HE IS NOT OUR TYPE OF A BUSINESSMAN. WE FEEL SORRY FOR YOU!
AND SO WE ARE OFFERING YOU A COTTAGE HOME IN THE SUBURBS, SO THAT YOU AND YOUR FAMILY CAN HAVE A NEW START IN LIFE - - - FREE FROM THE INFLU- ENCE OF YOUR AVARICIOUS UNCLE!
23

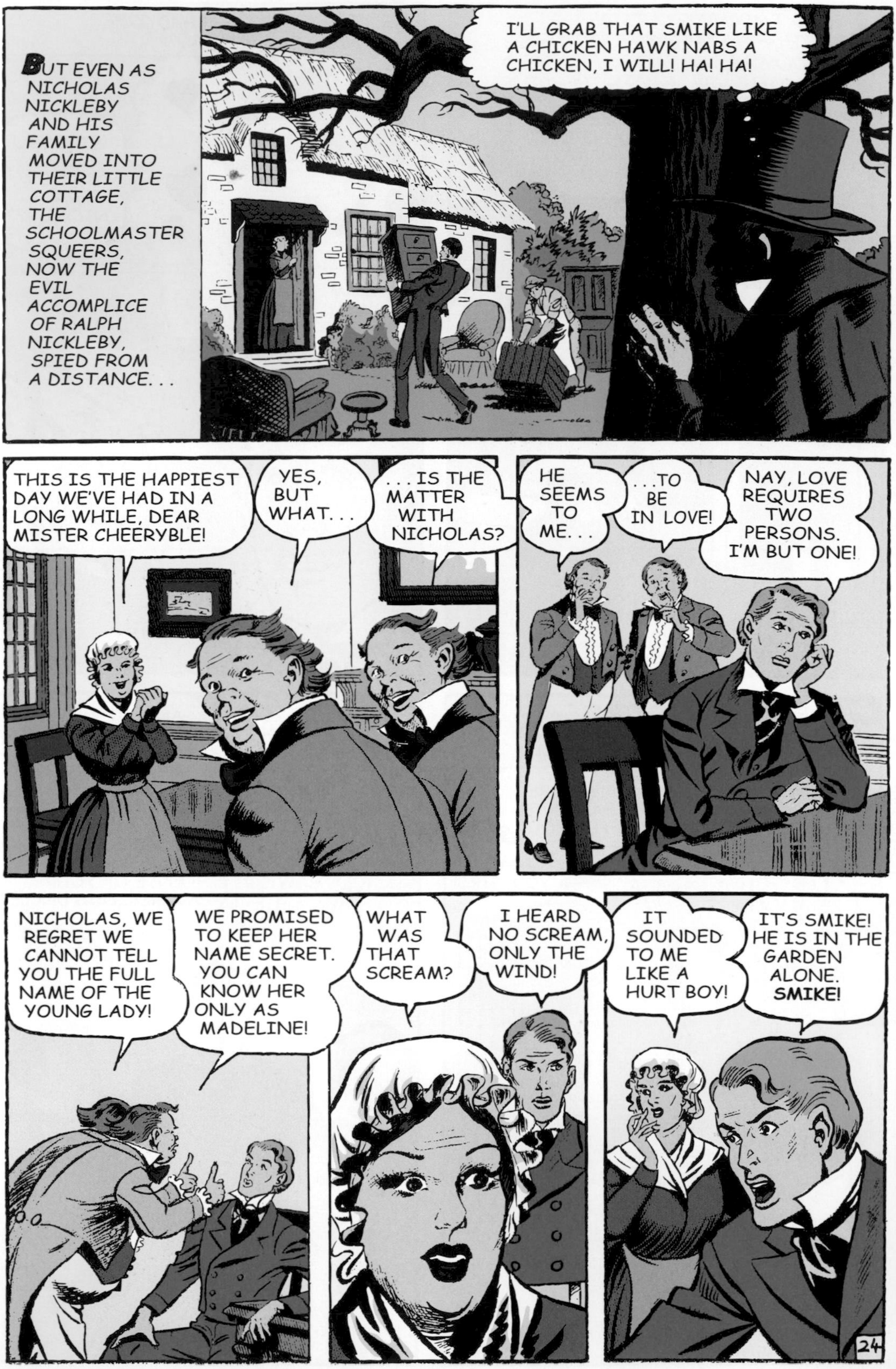
BUT EVEN AS NICHOLAS NICKLEBY AND HIS FAMILY MOVED INTO THEIR LITTLE COTTAGE, THE SCHOOLMASTER SQUEERS, NOW THE EVIL ACCOMPLICE OF RALPH NICKLEBY, SPIED FROM A DISTANCE. . .
I'LL GRAB THAT SMIKE LIKE A CHICKEN HAWK NABS A CHICKEN, I WILL! HA! HA!
THIS IS THE HAPPIEST DAY WE'VE HAD IN A LONG WHILE, DEAR MISTER CHEERYBLE!
YES, BUT WHAT. . .
. . . IS THE MATTER WITH NICHOLAS?
HE SEEMS TO ME. . .
. . .TO BE IN LOVE!
NAY, LOVE REQUIRES TWO PERSONS. I'M BUT ONE!
NICHOLAS, WE REGRET WE CANNOT TELL YOU THE FULL NAME OF THE YOUNG LADY!
WE PROMISED TO KEEP HER NAME SECRET. YOU CAN KNOW HER ONLY AS MADELINE!
WHAT WAS THAT SCREAM?
I HEARD NO SCREAM, ONLY THE WIND!
IT SOUNDED TO ME LIKE A HURT BOY!
IT'S SMIKE! HE IS IN THE GARDEN ALONE. SMIKE!
24

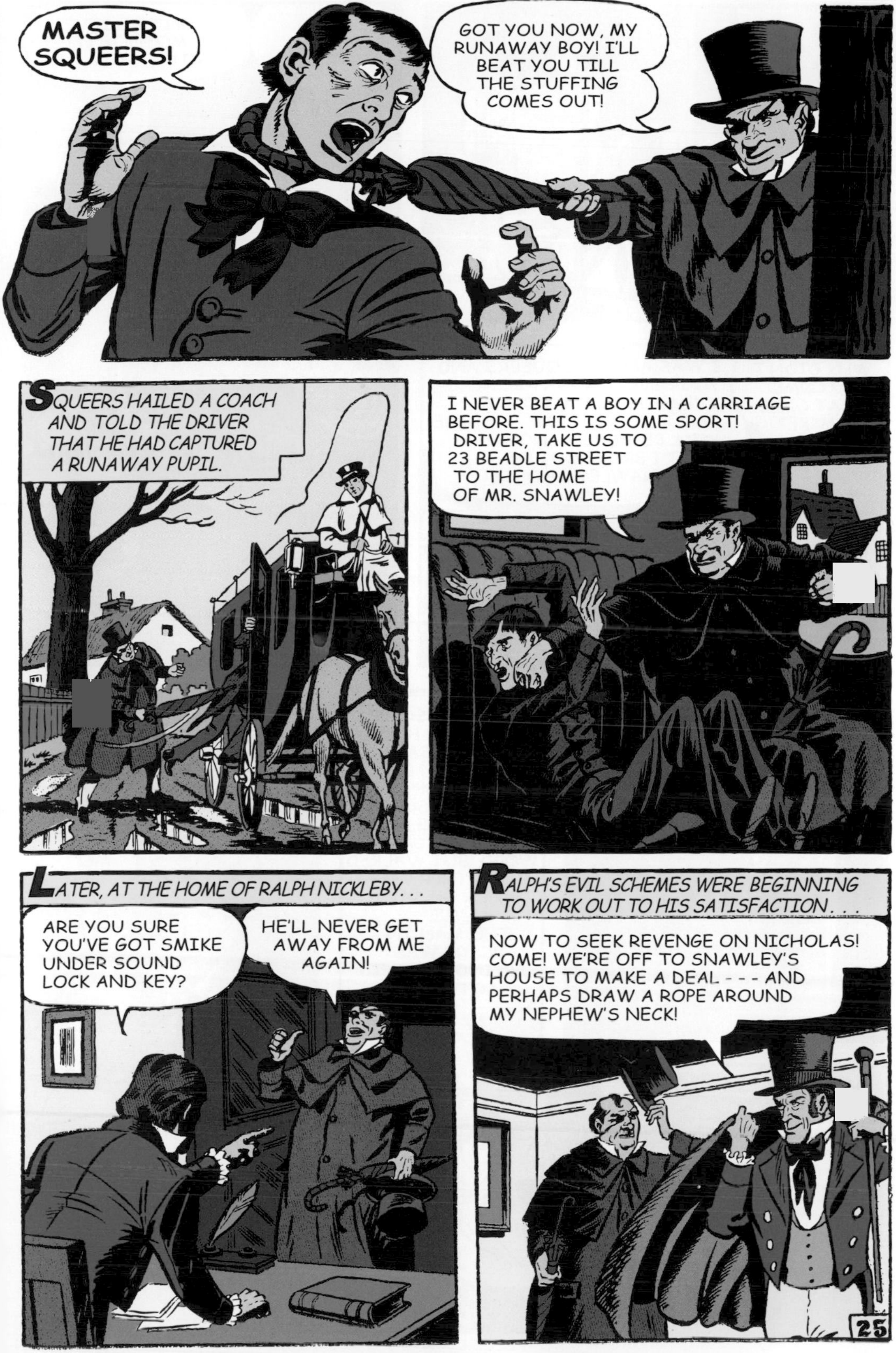
MASTER SQUEERS!
GOT YOU NOW, MY RUNAWAY BOY! I'LL BEAT YOU TILL THE STUFFING COMES OUT!
SQUEERS HAILED A COACH AND TOLD THE DRIVER THAT HE HAD CAPTURED A RUNAWAY PUPIL.
I NEVER BEAT A BOY IN A CARRIAGE BEFORE. THIS IS SOME SPORT! DRIVER, TAKE US TO 23 BEADLE STREET TO THE HOME OF MR. SNAWLEY!
LATER, AT THE HOME OF RALPH NICKLEBY. . .
ARE YOU SURE YOU'VE GOT SMIKE UNDER SOUND LOCK AND KEY?
HE'LL NEVER GET AWAY FROM ME AGAIN!
RALPH'S EVIL SCHEMES WERE BEGINNING TO WORK OUT TO HIS SATISFACTION . . .
NOW TO SEEK REVENGE ON NICHOLAS! COME! WE'RE OFF TO SNAWLEY'S HOUSE TO MAKE A DEAL - - - AND PERHAPS DRAW A ROPE AROUND MY NEPHEW'S NECK!
25

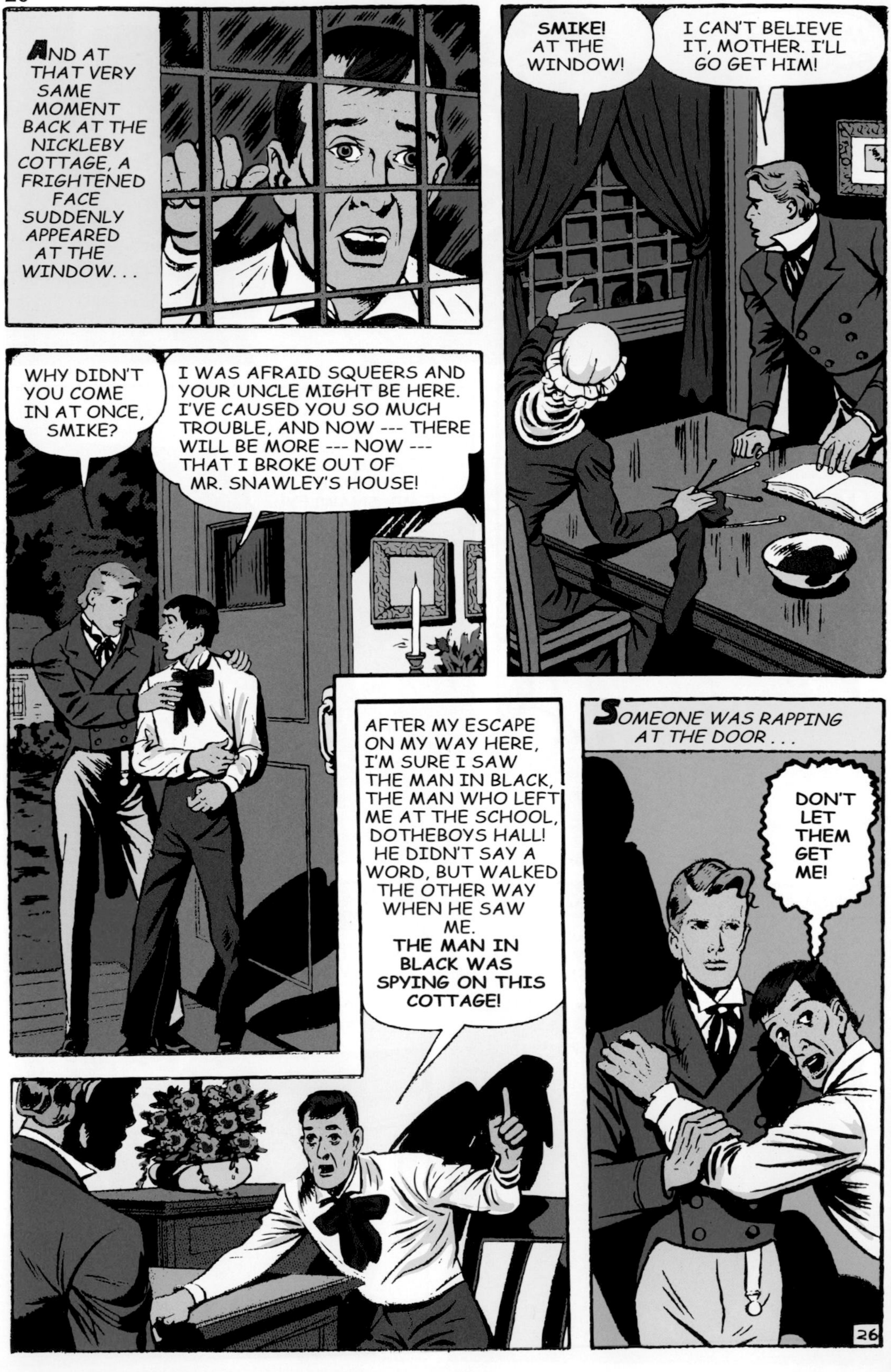
AND AT THAT VERY SAME MOMENT BACK AT THE NICKLEBY COTTAGE, A FRIGHTENED FACE SUDDENLY APPEARED AT THE WINDOW. . .
SMIKE! AT THE WINDOW!
I CAN'T BELIEVE IT, MOTHER. I'LL GO GET HIM!
WHY DIDN'T YOU COME IN AT ONCE, SMIKE?
I WAS AFRAID SQUEERS AND YOUR UNCLE MIGHT BE HERE. I'VE CAUSED YOU SO MUCH TROUBLE, AND NOW --- THERE WILL BE MORE --- NOW --- THAT I BROKE OUT OF MR. SNAWLEY'S HOUSE!
AFTER MY ESCAPE ON MY WAY HERE, I'M SURE I SAW THE MAN IN BLACK, THE MAN WHO LEFT ME AT THE SCHOOL, DOTHEBOYS HALL! HE DIDN'T SAY A WORD, BUT WALKED THE OTHER WAY WHEN HE SAW ME. THE MAN IN BLACK WAS SPYING ON THIS COTTAGE!
SOMEONE WAS RAPPING AT THE DOOR . . .
DON'T LET THEM GET ME!
26

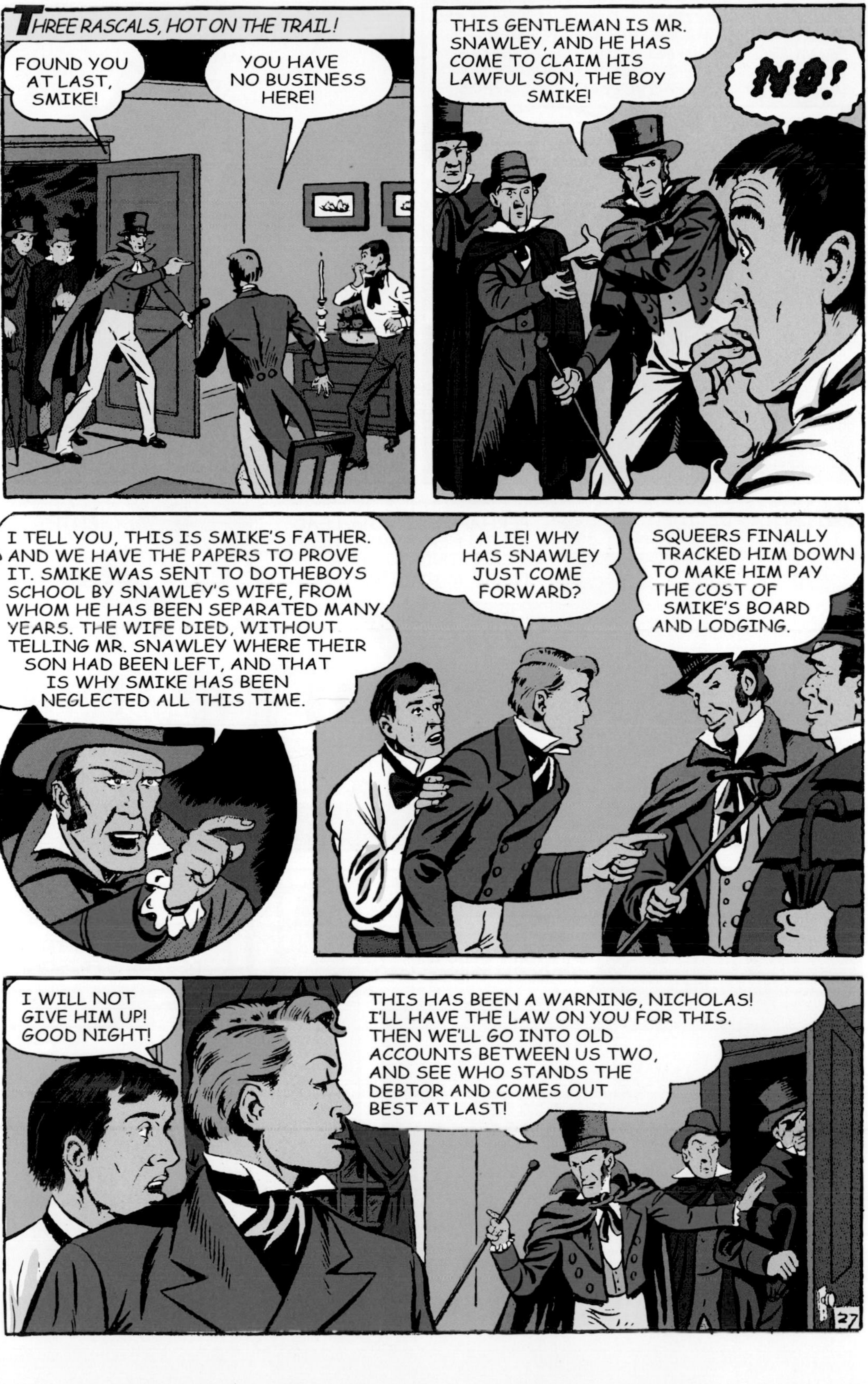
THREE RASCALS, HOT ON THE TRAIL!
FOUND YOU AT LAST, SMIKE!
YOU HAVE NO BUSINESS HERE!
THIS GENTLEMAN IS MR. SNAWLEY, AND HE HAS COME TO CLAIM HIS LAWFUL SON, THE BOY SMIKE!
NO!
I TELL YOU, THIS IS SMIKE'S FATHER. AND WE HAVE THE PAPERS TO PROVE IT. SMIKE WAS SENT TO DOTHEBOYS SCHOOL BY SNAWLEY'S WIFE, FROM WHOM HE HAS BEEN SEPARATED MANY YEARS. THE WIFE DIED, WITHOUT TELLING MR. SNAWLEY WHERE THEIR SON HAD BEEN LEFT, AND THAT IS WHY SMIKE HAS BEEN NEGLECTED ALL THIS TIME.
A LIE! WHY HAS SNAWLEY JUST COME FORWARD?
SQUEERS FINALLY TRACKED HIM DOWN TO MAKE HIM PAY THE COST OF SMIKE'S BOARD AND LODGING.
I WILL NOT GIVE HIM UP! GOOD NIGHT!
THIS HAS BEEN A WARNING, NICHOLAS! I'LL HAVE THE LAW ON YOU FOR THIS. THEN WE'LL GO INTO OLD ACCOUNTS BETWEEN US TWO, AND SEE WHO STANDS THE DEBTOR AND COMES OUT BEST AT LAST!
27

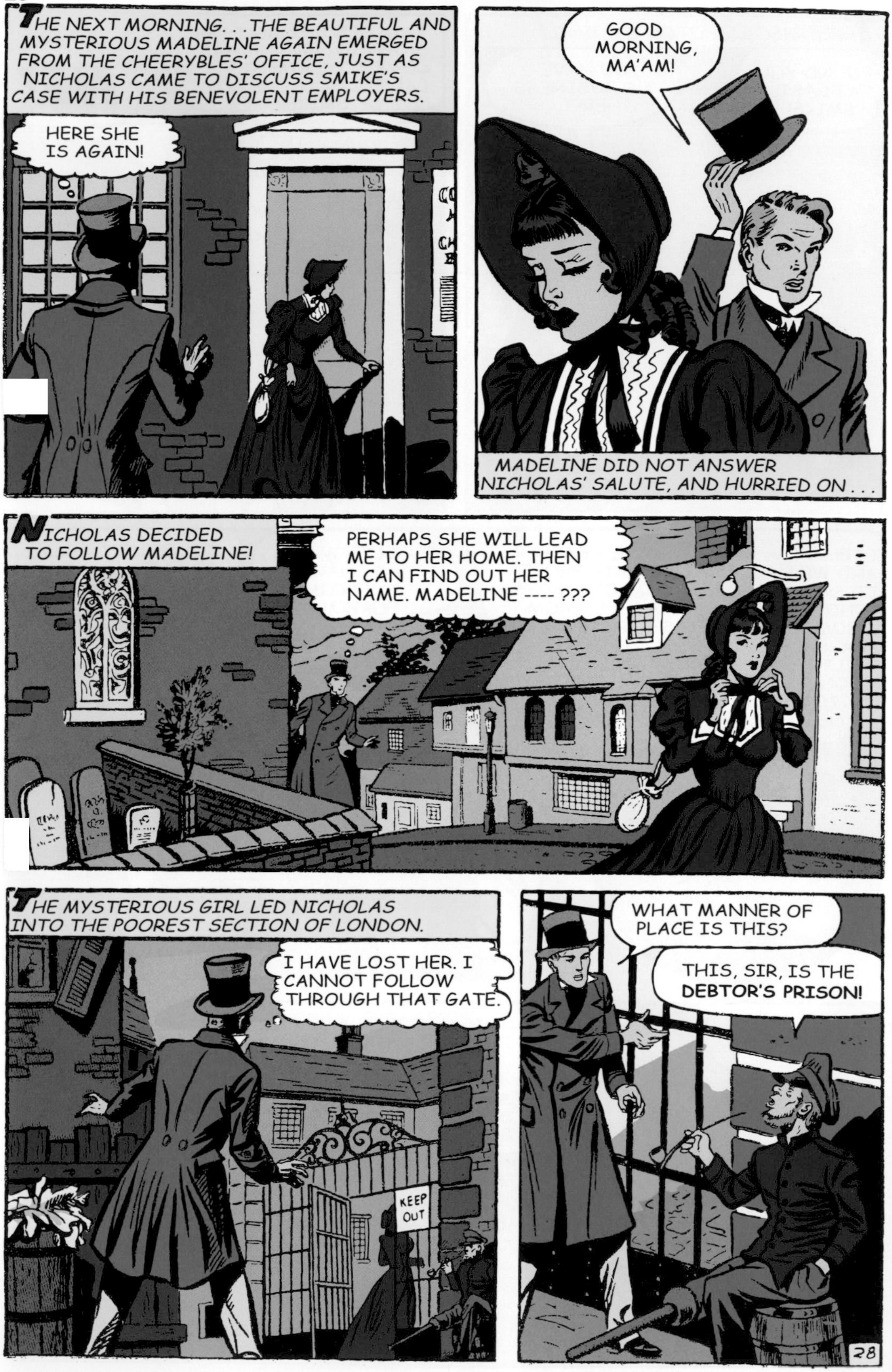
THE NEXT MORNING. . .THE BEAUTIFUL AND MYSTERIOUS MADELINE AGAIN EMERGED FROM THE CHEERYBLES' OFFICE, JUST AS NICHOLAS CAME TO DISCUSS SMIKE'S CASE WITH HIS BENEVOLENT EMPLOYERS.
HERE SHE IS AGAIN!
GOOD MORNING, MA'AM!
MADELINE DID NOT ANSWER NICHOLAS' SALUTE, AND HURRIED ON . . .
NICHOLAS DECIDED TO FOLLOW MADELINE!
PERHAPS SHE WILL LEAD ME TO HER HOME. THEN I CAN FIND OUT HER NAME. MADELINE ---- ???
THE MYSTERIOUS GIRL LED NICHOLAS INTO THE POOREST SECTION OF LONDON.
I HAVE LOST HER. I CANNOT FOLLOW THROUGH THAT GATE.
KEEP OUT
WHAT MANNER OF PLACE IS THIS?
THIS, SIR, IS THE **DEBTOR'S PRISON!**
28

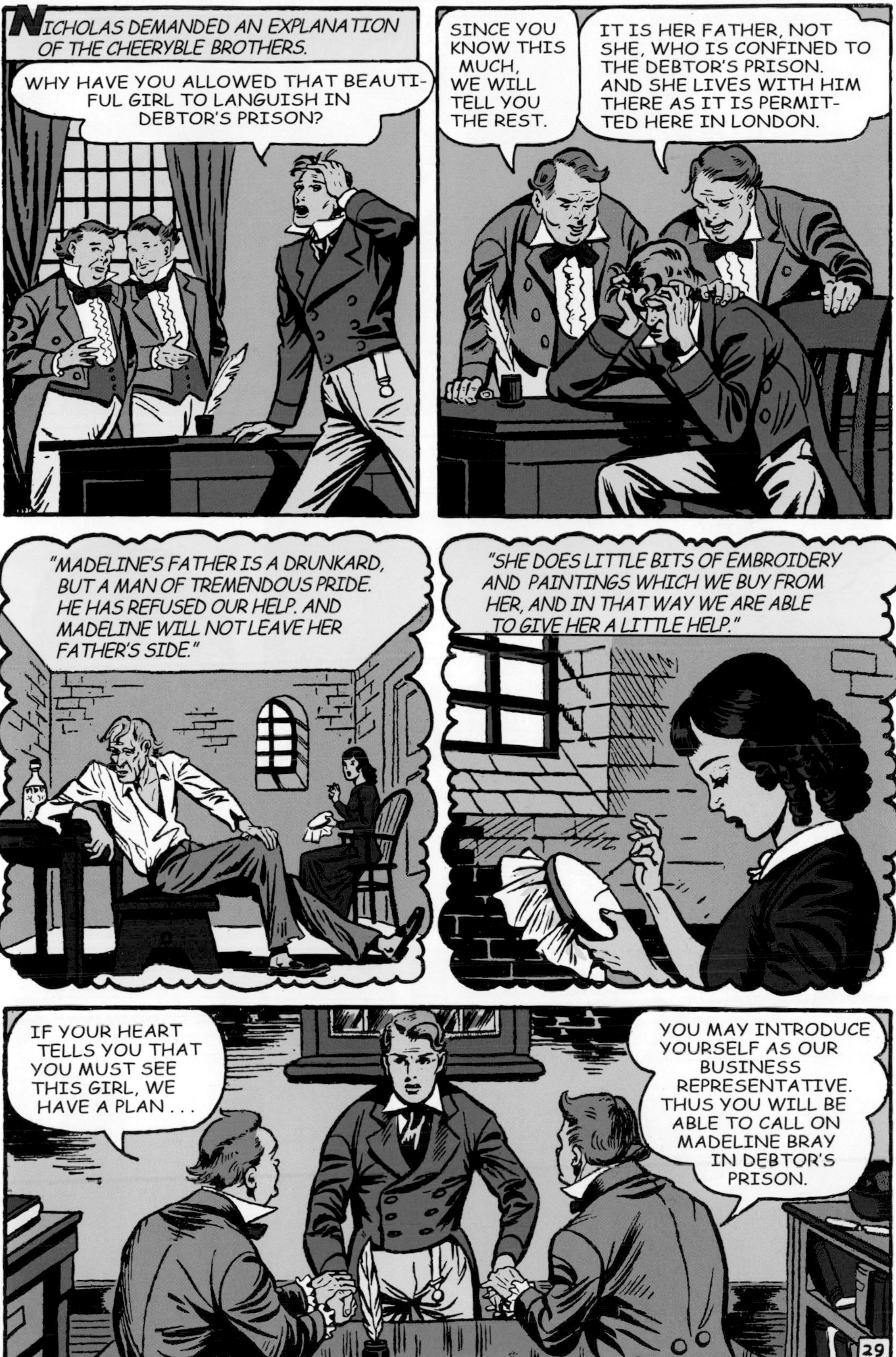
NICHOLAS DEMANDED AN EXPLANATION OF THE CHEERYBLE BROTHERS.
WHY HAVE YOU ALLOWED THAT BEAUTIFUL GIRL TO LANGUISH IN DEBTOR'S PRISON?
SINCE YOU KNOW THIS MUCH, WE WILL TELL YOU THE REST.
IT IS HER FATHER, NOT SHE, WHO IS CONFINED TO THE DEBTOR'S PRISON. AND SHE LIVES WITH HIM THERE AS IT IS PERMITTED HERE IN LONDON.
"MADELINE'S FATHER IS A DRUNKARD, BUT A MAN OF TREMENDOUS PRIDE. HE HAS REFUSED OUR HELP. AND MADELINE WILL NOT LEAVE HER FATHER'S SIDE."
"SHE DOES LITTLE BITS OF EMBROIDERY AND PAINTINGS WHICH WE BUY FROM HER, AND IN THAT WAY WE ARE ABLE TO GIVE HER A LITTLE HELP."
IF YOUR HEART TELLS YOU THAT YOU MUST SEE THIS GIRL, WE HAVE A PLAN . . .
YOU MAY INTRODUCE YOURSELF AS OUR BUSINESS REPRESENTATIVE. THUS YOU WILL BE ABLE TO CALL ON MADELINE BRAY IN DEBTOR'S PRISON.
29

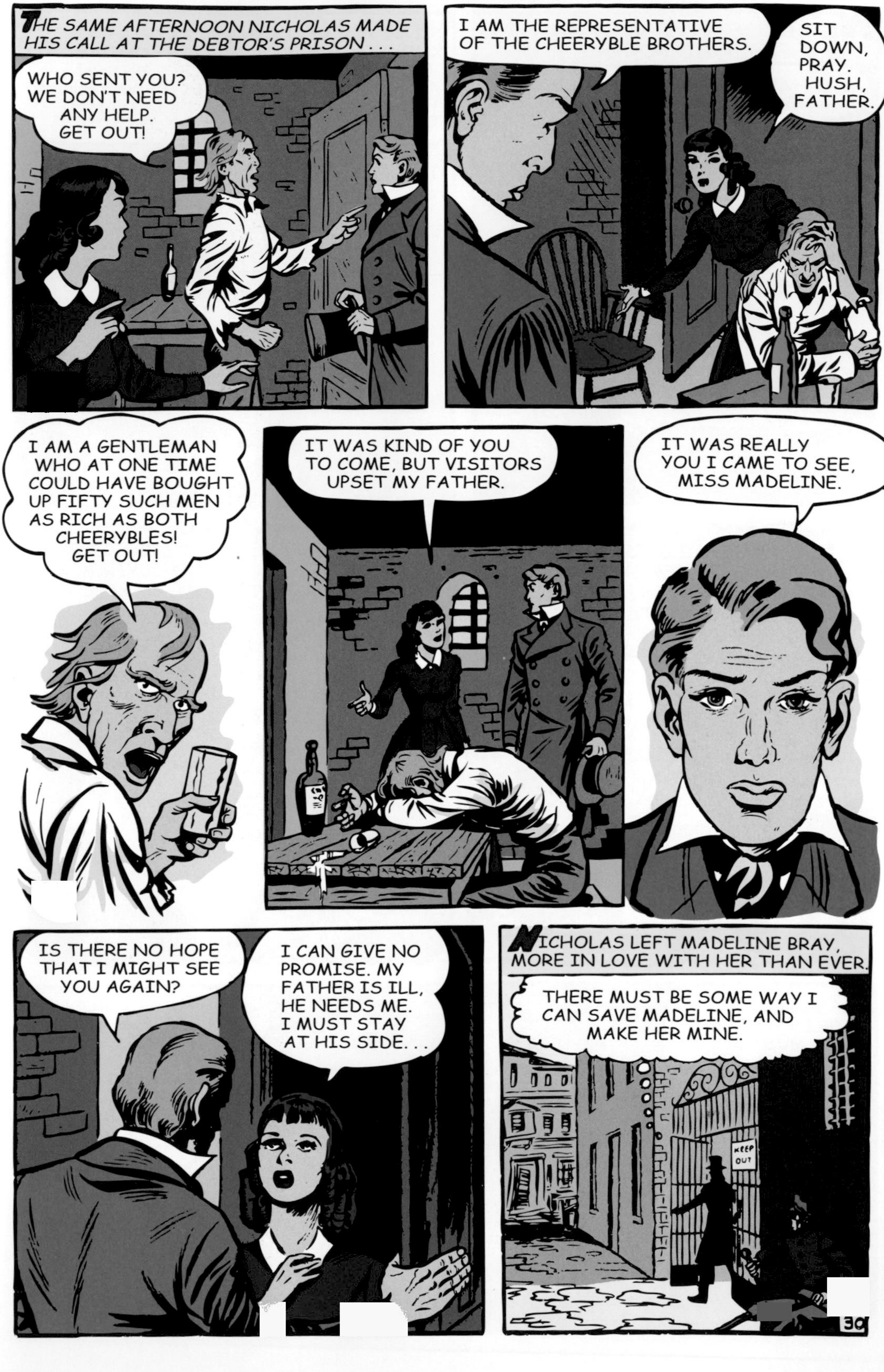
THE SAME AFTERNOON NICHOLAS MADE HIS CALL AT THE DEBTOR'S PRISON . . .
WHO SENT YOU? WE DON'T NEED ANY HELP. GET OUT!
I AM THE REPRESENTATIVE OF THE CHEERYBLE BROTHERS.
SIT DOWN, PRAY. HUSH, FATHER.
I AM A GENTLEMAN WHO AT ONE TIME COULD HAVE BOUGHT UP FIFTY SUCH MEN AS RICH AS BOTH CHEERYBLES! GET OUT!
IT WAS KIND OF YOU TO COME, BUT VISITORS UPSET MY FATHER.
IT WAS REALLY YOU I CAME TO SEE, MISS MADELINE.
IS THERE NO HOPE THAT I MIGHT SEE YOU AGAIN?
I CAN GIVE NO PROMISE. MY FATHER IS ILL, HE NEEDS ME. I MUST STAY AT HIS SIDE. . .
NICHOLAS LEFT MADELINE BRAY, MORE IN LOVE WITH HER THAN EVER.
THERE MUST BE SOME WAY I CAN SAVE MADELINE, AND MAKE HER MINE.
KEEP OUT
30

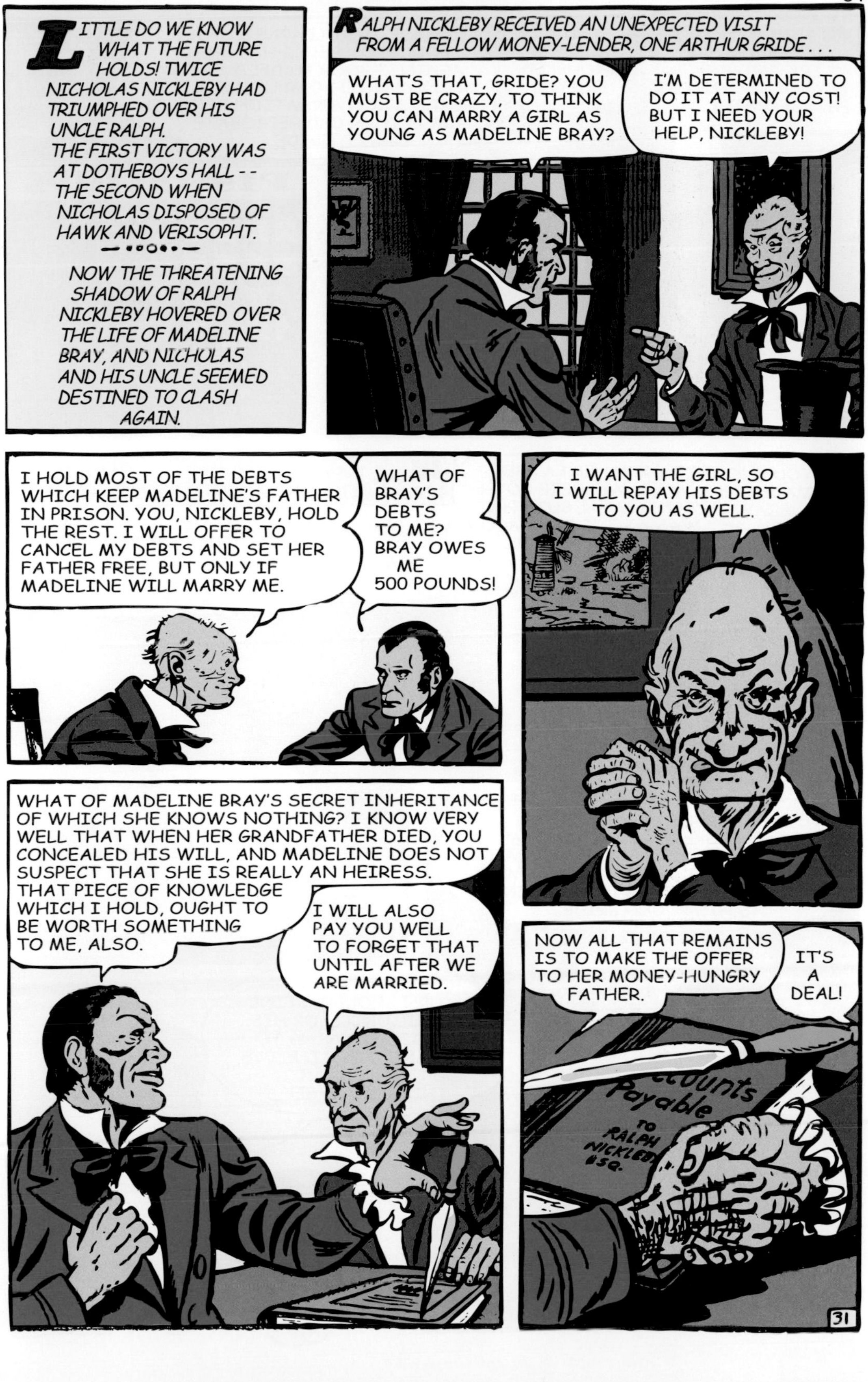
LITTLE DO WE KNOW WHAT THE FUTURE HOLDS! TWICE NICHOLAS NICKLEBY HAD TRIUMPHED OVER HIS UNCLE RALPH. THE FIRST VICTORY WAS AT DOTHEBOYS HALL - - THE SECOND WHEN NICHOLAS DISPOSED OF HAWK AND VERISOPHT.
NOW THE THREATENING SHADOW OF RALPH NICKLEBY HOVERED OVER THE LIFE OF MADELINE BRAY, AND NICHOLAS AND HIS UNCLE SEEMED DESTINED TO CLASH AGAIN.
RALPH NICKLEBY RECEIVED AN UNEXPECTED VISIT FROM A FELLOW MONEY-LENDER, ONE ARTHUR GRIDE . . .
WHAT'S THAT, GRIDE? YOU MUST BE CRAZY, TO THINK YOU CAN MARRY A GIRL AS YOUNG AS MADELINE BRAY?
I'M DETERMINED TO DO IT AT ANY COST! BUT I NEED YOUR HELP, NICKLEBY!
I HOLD MOST OF THE DEBTS WHICH KEEP MADELINE'S FATHER IN PRISON. YOU, NICKLEBY, HOLD THE REST. I WILL OFFER TO CANCEL MY DEBTS AND SET HER FATHER FREE, BUT ONLY IF MADELINE WILL MARRY ME.
WHAT OF BRAY'S DEBTS TO ME? BRAY OWES ME 500 POUNDS!
I WANT THE GIRL, SO I WILL REPAY HIS DEBTS TO YOU AS WELL.
WHAT OF MADELINE BRAY'S SECRET INHERITANCE OF WHICH SHE KNOWS NOTHING? I KNOW VERY WELL THAT WHEN HER GRANDFATHER DIED, YOU CONCEALED HIS WILL, AND MADELINE DOES NOT SUSPECT THAT SHE IS REALLY AN HEIRESS. THAT PIECE OF KNOWLEDGE WHICH I HOLD, OUGHT TO BE WORTH SOMETHING TO ME, ALSO.
I WILL ALSO PAY YOU WELL TO FORGET THAT UNTIL AFTER WE ARE MARRIED.
NOW ALL THAT REMAINS IS TO MAKE THE OFFER TO HER MONEY-HUNGRY FATHER.
IT'S A DEAL!
Accounts Payable TO RALPH NICKLEBY ESQ.
31

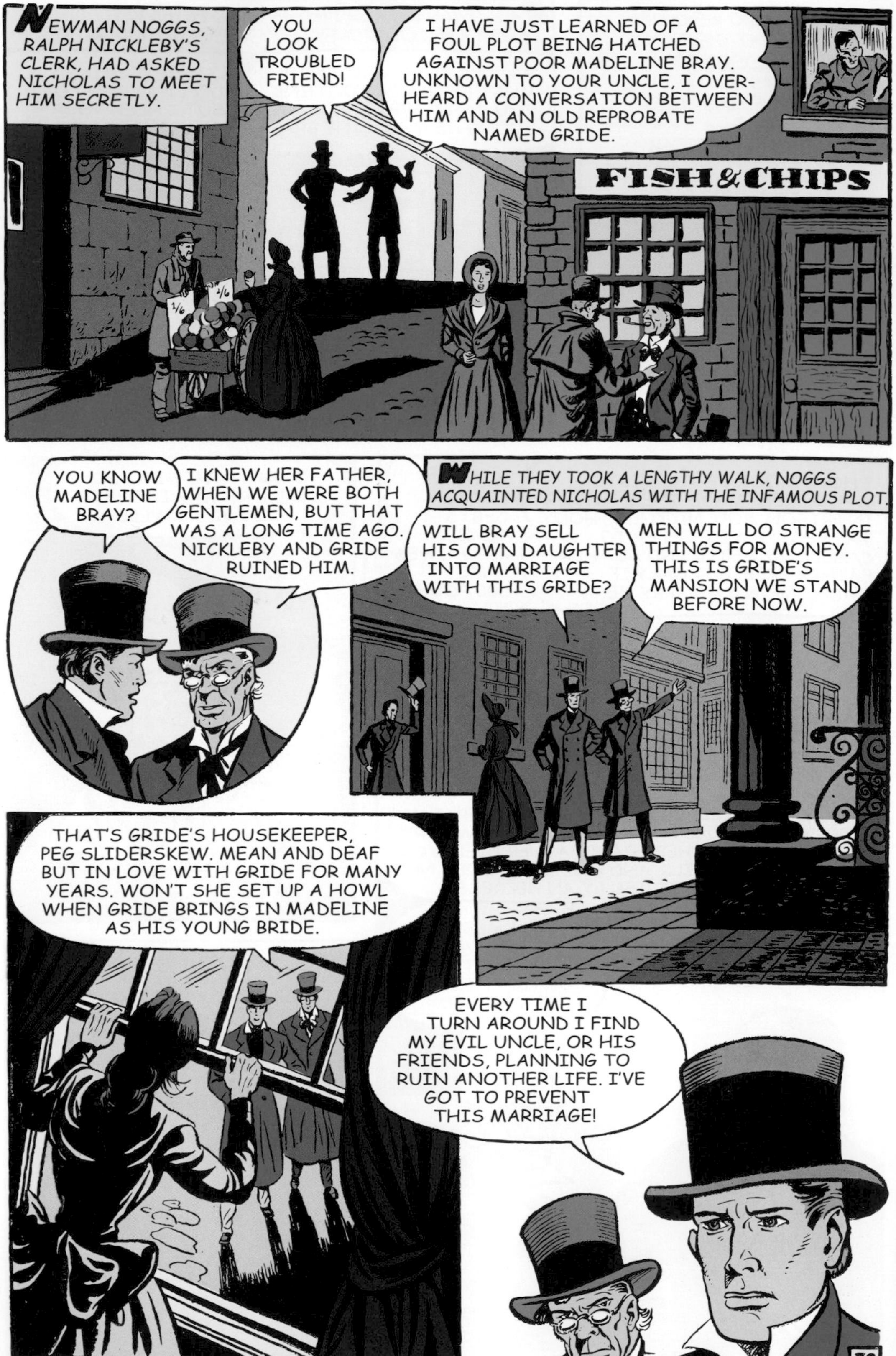
NEWMAN NOGGS, RALPH NICKLEBY'S CLERK, HAD ASKED NICHOLAS TO MEET HIM SECRETLY.
YOU LOOK TROUBLED FRIEND!
I HAVE JUST LEARNED OF A FOUL PLOT BEING HATCHED AGAINST POOR MADELINE BRAY. UNKNOWN TO YOUR UNCLE, I OVER-HEARD A CONVERSATION BETWEEN HIM AND AN OLD REPROBATE NAMED GRIDE.
FISH & CHIPS
YOU KNOW MADELINE BRAY?
I KNEW HER FATHER, WHEN WE WERE BOTH GENTLEMEN, BUT THAT WAS A LONG TIME AGO. NICKLEBY AND GRIDE RUINED HIM.
WHILE THEY TOOK A LENGTHY WALK, NOGGS ACQUAINTED NICHOLAS WITH THE INFAMOUS PLOT.
WILL BRAY SELL HIS OWN DAUGHTER INTO MARRIAGE WITH THIS GRIDE?
MEN WILL DO STRANGE THINGS FOR MONEY. THIS IS GRIDE'S MANSION WE STAND BEFORE NOW.
THAT'S GRIDE'S HOUSEKEEPER, PEG SLIDERSKEW. MEAN AND DEAF BUT IN LOVE WITH GRIDE FOR MANY YEARS. WON'T SHE SET UP A HOWL WHEN GRIDE BRINGS IN MADELINE AS HIS YOUNG BRIDE.
EVERY TIME I TURN AROUND I FIND MY EVIL UNCLE, OR HIS FRIENDS, PLANNING TO RUIN ANOTHER LIFE. I'VE GOT TO PREVENT THIS MARRIAGE!
32

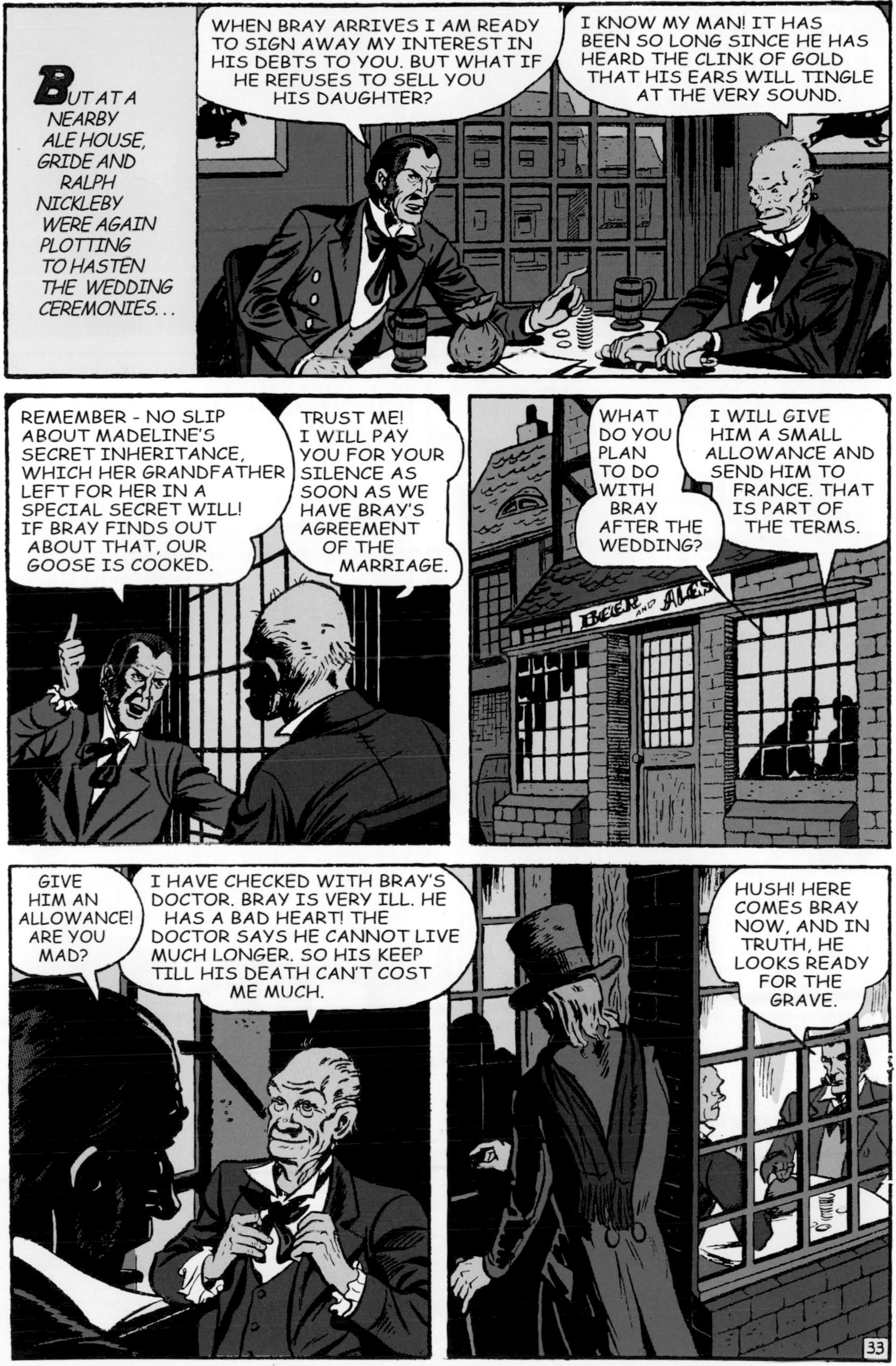
BUT AT A NEARBY ALE HOUSE, GRIDE AND RALPH NICKLEBY WERE AGAIN PLOTTING TO HASTEN THE WEDDING CEREMONIES...
WHEN BRAY ARRIVES I AM READY TO SIGN AWAY MY INTEREST IN HIS DEBTS TO YOU. BUT WHAT IF HE REFUSES TO SELL YOU HIS DAUGHTER?
I KNOW MY MAN! IT HAS BEEN SO LONG SINCE HE HAS HEARD THE CLINK OF GOLD THAT HIS EARS WILL TINGLE AT THE VERY SOUND.
REMEMBER - NO SLIP ABOUT MADELINE'S SECRET INHERITANCE, WHICH HER GRANDFATHER LEFT FOR HER IN A SPECIAL SECRET WILL! IF BRAY FINDS OUT ABOUT THAT, OUR GOOSE IS COOKED.
TRUST ME! I WILL PAY YOU FOR YOUR SILENCE AS SOON AS WE HAVE BRAY'S AGREEMENT OF THE MARRIAGE.
WHAT DO YOU PLAN TO DO WITH BRAY AFTER THE WEDDING?
I WILL GIVE HIM A SMALL ALLOWANCE AND SEND HIM TO FRANCE. THAT IS PART OF THE TERMS.
BEER AND ALES
GIVE HIM AN ALLOWANCE! ARE YOU MAD?
I HAVE CHECKED WITH BRAY'S DOCTOR. BRAY IS VERY ILL. HE HAS A BAD HEART! THE DOCTOR SAYS HE CANNOT LIVE MUCH LONGER. SO HIS KEEP TILL HIS DEATH CAN'T COST ME MUCH.
HUSH! HERE COMES BRAY NOW, AND IN TRUTH, HE LOOKS READY FOR THE GRAVE.
33

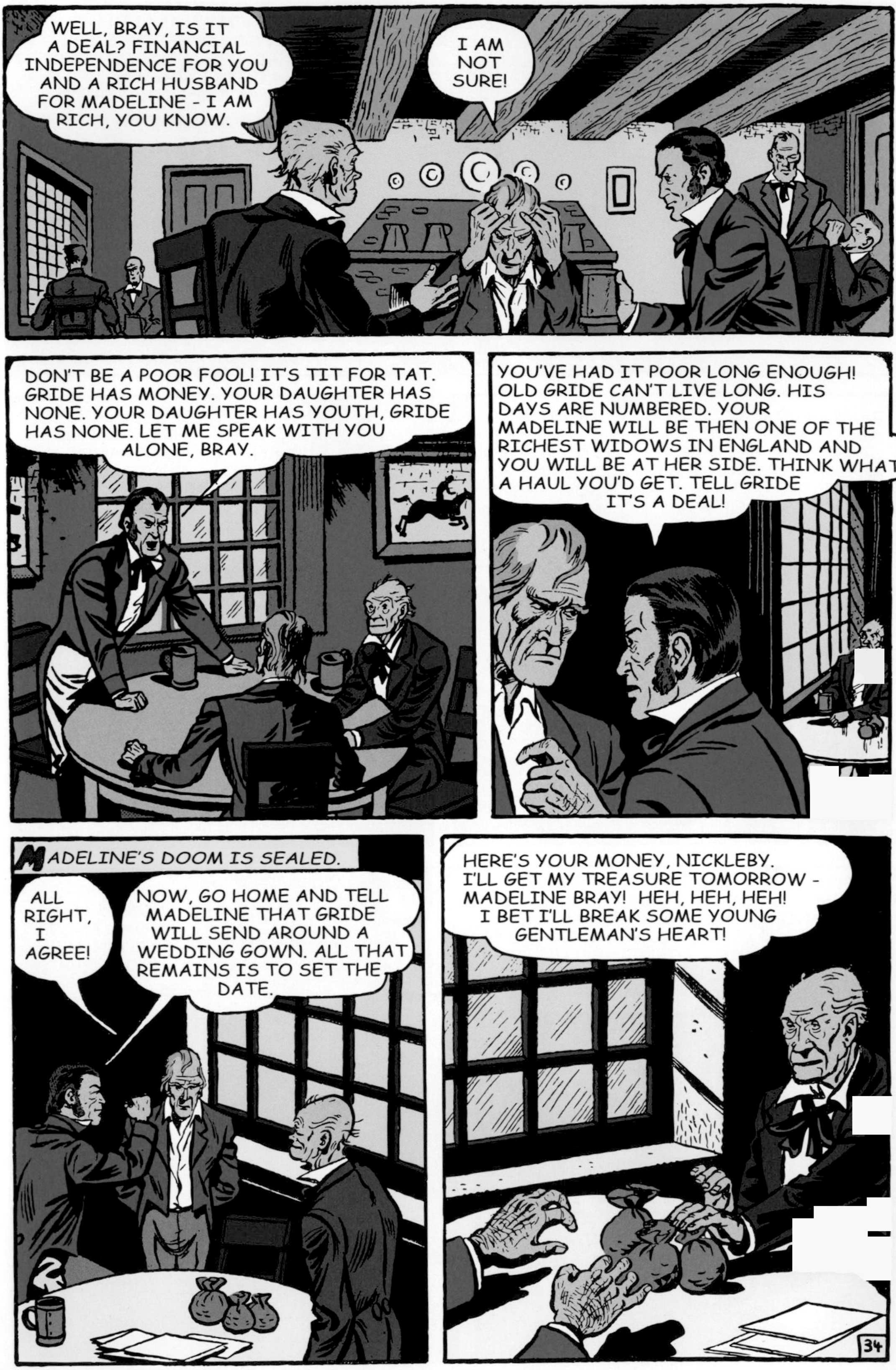
WELL, BRAY, IS IT A DEAL? FINANCIAL INDEPENDENCE FOR YOU AND A RICH HUSBAND FOR MADELINE - I AM RICH, YOU KNOW.
I AM NOT SURE!
DON'T BE A POOR FOOL! IT'S TIT FOR TAT. GRIDE HAS MONEY. YOUR DAUGHTER HAS NONE. YOUR DAUGHTER HAS YOUTH, GRIDE HAS NONE. LET ME SPEAK WITH YOU ALONE, BRAY.
YOU'VE HAD IT POOR LONG ENOUGH! OLD GRIDE CAN'T LIVE LONG. HIS DAYS ARE NUMBERED. YOUR MADELINE WILL BE THEN ONE OF THE RICHEST WIDOWS IN ENGLAND AND YOU WILL BE AT HER SIDE. THINK WHAT A HAUL YOU'D GET. TELL GRIDE IT'S A DEAL!
MADELINE'S DOOM IS SEALED.
ALL RIGHT, I AGREE!
NOW, GO HOME AND TELL MADELINE THAT GRIDE WILL SEND AROUND A WEDDING GOWN. ALL THAT REMAINS IS TO SET THE DATE.
HERE'S YOUR MONEY, NICKLEBY. I'LL GET MY TREASURE TOMORROW - MADELINE BRAY! HEH, HEH, HEH! I BET I'LL BREAK SOME YOUNG GENTLEMAN'S HEART!
34

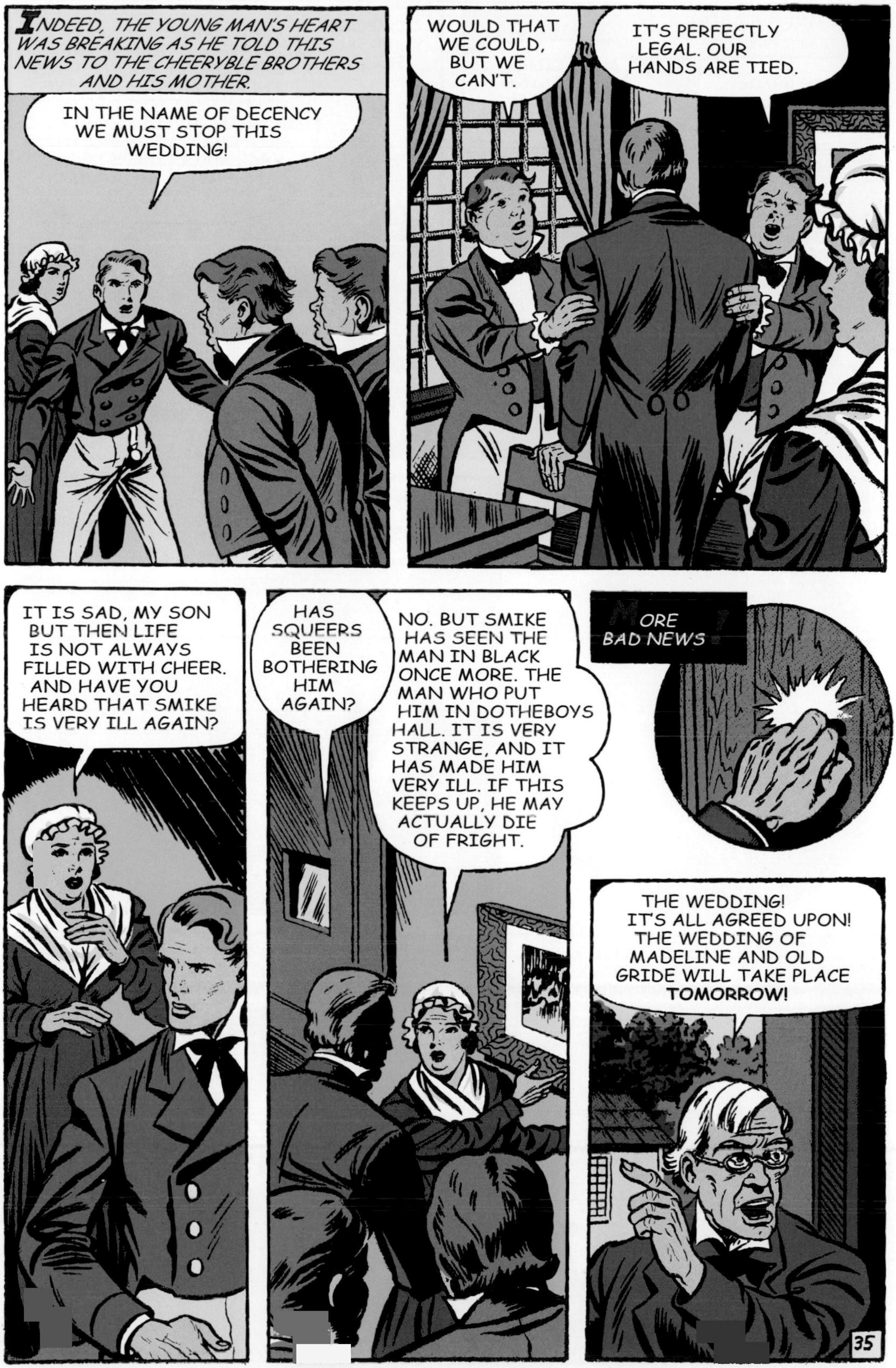
INDEED, THE YOUNG MAN'S HEART WAS BREAKING AS HE TOLD THIS NEWS TO THE CHEERYBLE BROTHERS AND HIS MOTHER.
IN THE NAME OF DECENCY WE MUST STOP THIS WEDDING!
WOULD THAT WE COULD, BUT WE CAN'T.
IT'S PERFECTLY LEGAL. OUR HANDS ARE TIED.
IT IS SAD, MY SON BUT THEN LIFE IS NOT ALWAYS FILLED WITH CHEER. AND HAVE YOU HEARD THAT SMIKE IS VERY ILL AGAIN?
HAS SQUEERS BEEN BOTHERING HIM AGAIN?
NO. BUT SMIKE HAS SEEN THE MAN IN BLACK ONCE MORE. THE MAN WHO PUT HIM IN DOTHEBOYS HALL. IT IS VERY STRANGE, AND IT HAS MADE HIM VERY ILL. IF THIS KEEPS UP, HE MAY ACTUALLY DIE OF FRIGHT.
MORE BAD NEWS
THE WEDDING! IT'S ALL AGREED UPON! THE WEDDING OF MADELINE AND OLD GRIDE WILL TAKE PLACE TOMORROW!
35

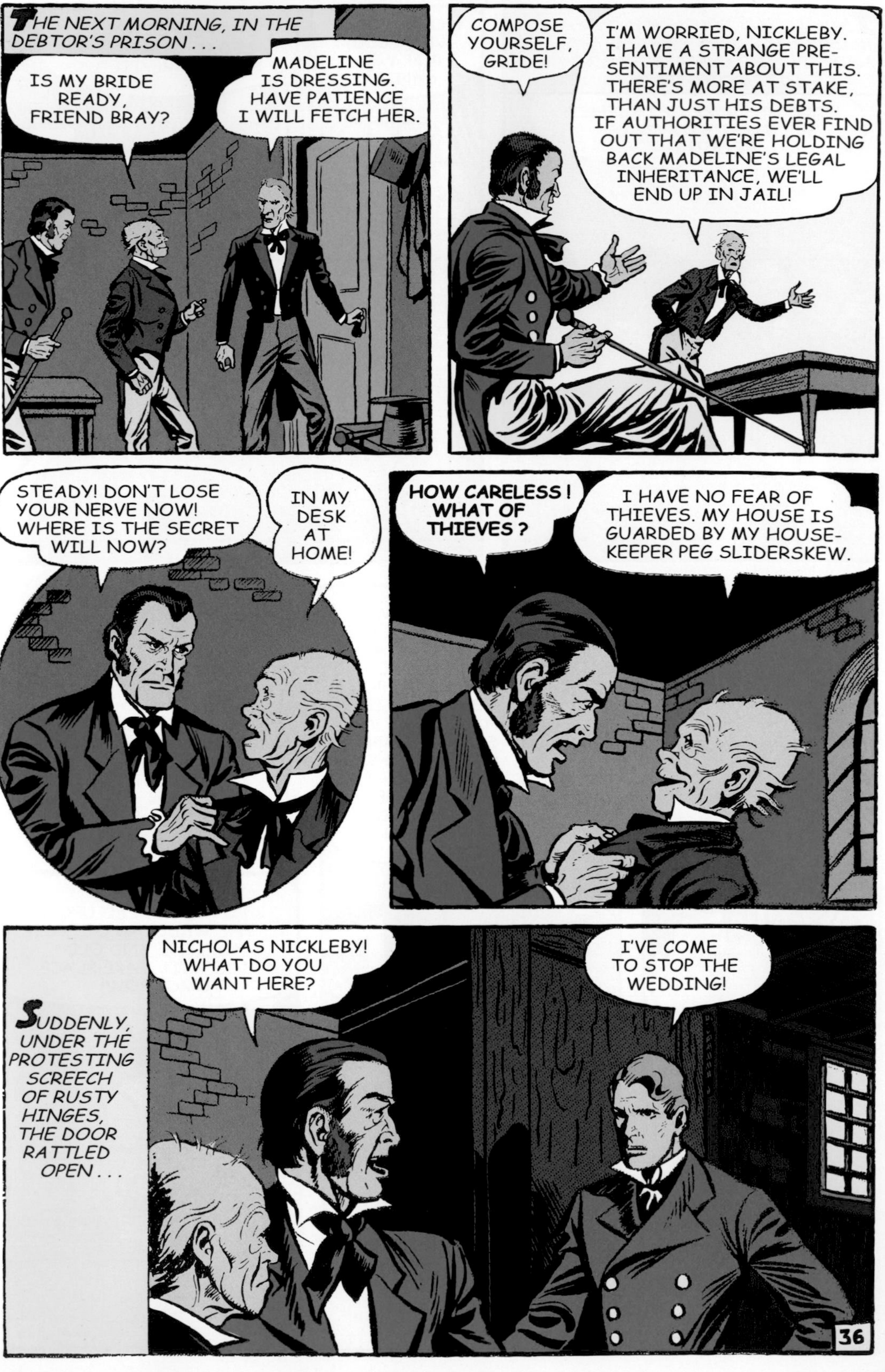
THE NEXT MORNING, IN THE DEBTOR'S PRISON . . .
IS MY BRIDE READY, FRIEND BRAY?
MADELINE IS DRESSING. HAVE PATIENCE I WILL FETCH HER.
COMPOSE YOURSELF, GRIDE!
I'M WORRIED, NICKLEBY. I HAVE A STRANGE PRESENTIMENT ABOUT THIS. THERE'S MORE AT STAKE, THAN JUST HIS DEBTS. IF AUTHORITIES EVER FIND OUT THAT WE'RE HOLDING BACK MADELINE'S LEGAL INHERITANCE, WE'LL END UP IN JAIL!
STEADY! DON'T LOSE YOUR NERVE NOW! WHERE IS THE SECRET WILL NOW?
IN MY DESK AT HOME!
HOW CARELESS ! WHAT OF THIEVES ?
I HAVE NO FEAR OF THIEVES. MY HOUSE IS GUARDED BY MY HOUSEKEEPER PEG SLIDERSKEW.
SUDDENLY, UNDER THE PROTESTING SCREECH OF RUSTY HINGES, THE DOOR RATTLED OPEN . . .
NICHOLAS NICKLEBY! WHAT DO YOU WANT HERE?
I'VE COME TO STOP THE WEDDING!
36

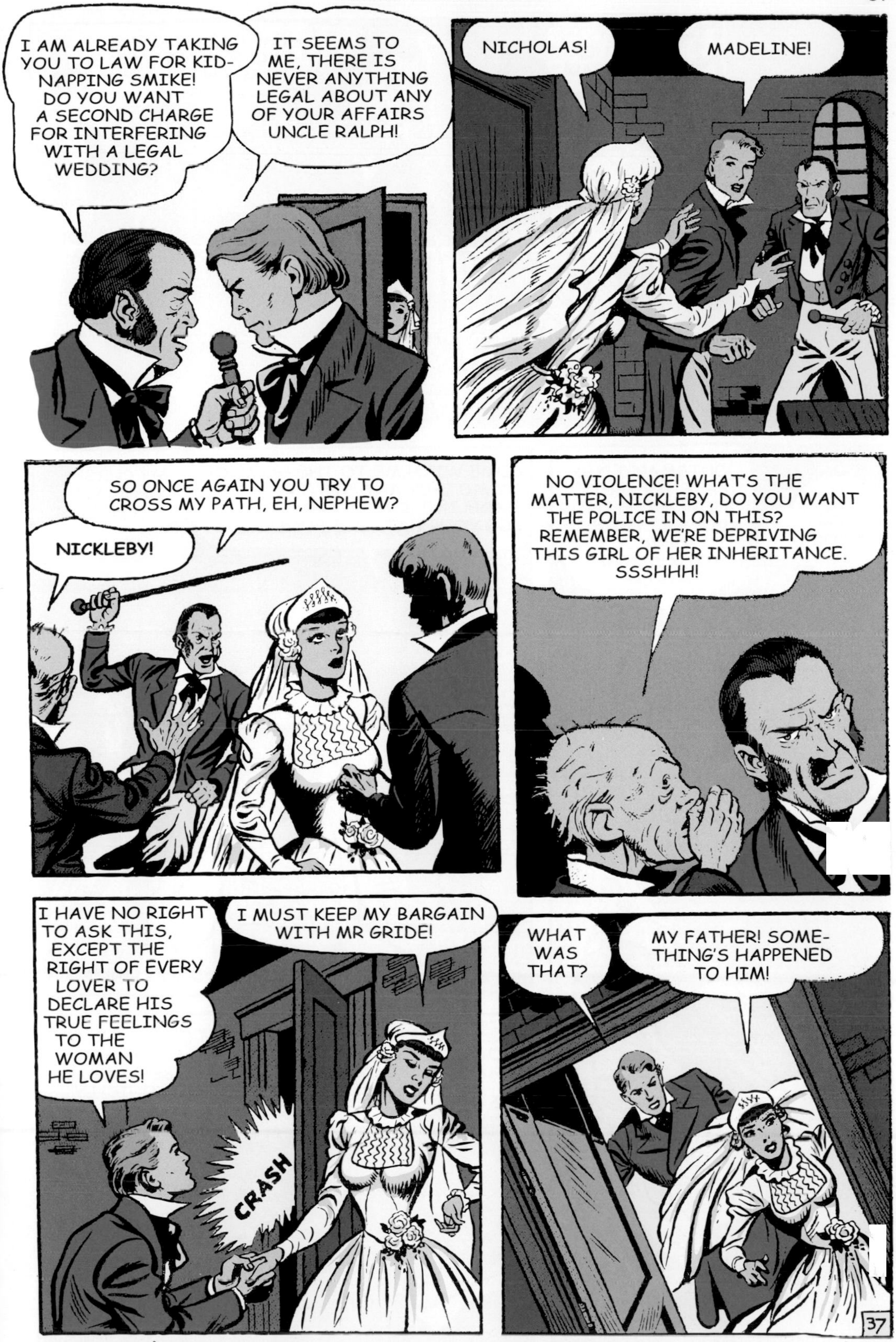
I AM ALREADY TAKING YOU TO LAW FOR KID-NAPPING SMIKE! DO YOU WANT A SECOND CHARGE FOR INTERFERING WITH A LEGAL WEDDING?
IT SEEMS TO ME, THERE IS NEVER ANYTHING LEGAL ABOUT ANY OF YOUR AFFAIRS UNCLE RALPH!
NICHOLAS!
MADELINE!
NICKLEBY!
SO ONCE AGAIN YOU TRY TO CROSS MY PATH, EH, NEPHEW?
NO VIOLENCE! WHAT'S THE MATTER, NICKLEBY, DO YOU WANT THE POLICE IN ON THIS? REMEMBER, WE'RE DEPRIVING THIS GIRL OF HER INHERITANCE. SSSHHH!
I HAVE NO RIGHT TO ASK THIS, EXCEPT THE RIGHT OF EVERY LOVER TO DECLARE HIS TRUE FEELINGS TO THE WOMAN HE LOVES!
I MUST KEEP MY BARGAIN WITH MR GRIDE!
CRASH
WHAT WAS THAT?
MY FATHER! SOME-THING'S HAPPENED TO HIM!
37

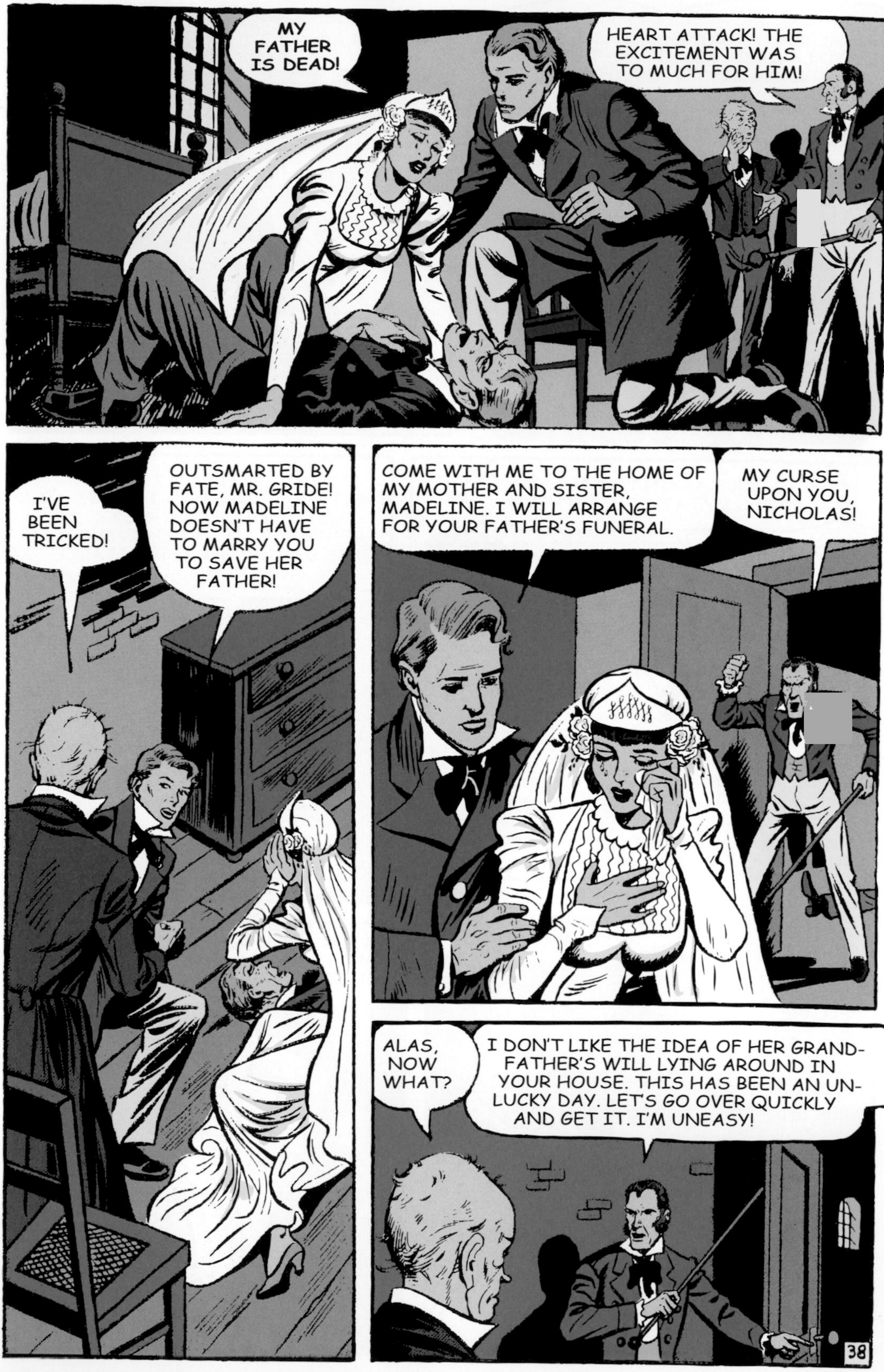
MY FATHER IS DEAD!
HEART ATTACK! THE EXCITEMENT WAS TO MUCH FOR HIM!
I'VE BEEN TRICKED!
OUTSMARTED BY FATE, MR. GRIDE! NOW MADELINE DOESN'T HAVE TO MARRY YOU TO SAVE HER FATHER!
COME WITH ME TO THE HOME OF MY MOTHER AND SISTER, MADELINE. I WILL ARRANGE FOR YOUR FATHER'S FUNERAL.
MY CURSE UPON YOU, NICHOLAS!
ALAS, NOW WHAT?
I DON'T LIKE THE IDEA OF HER GRAND-FATHER'S WILL LYING AROUND IN YOUR HOUSE. THIS HAS BEEN AN UN-LUCKY DAY. LET'S GO OVER QUICKLY AND GET IT. I'M UNEASY!
38

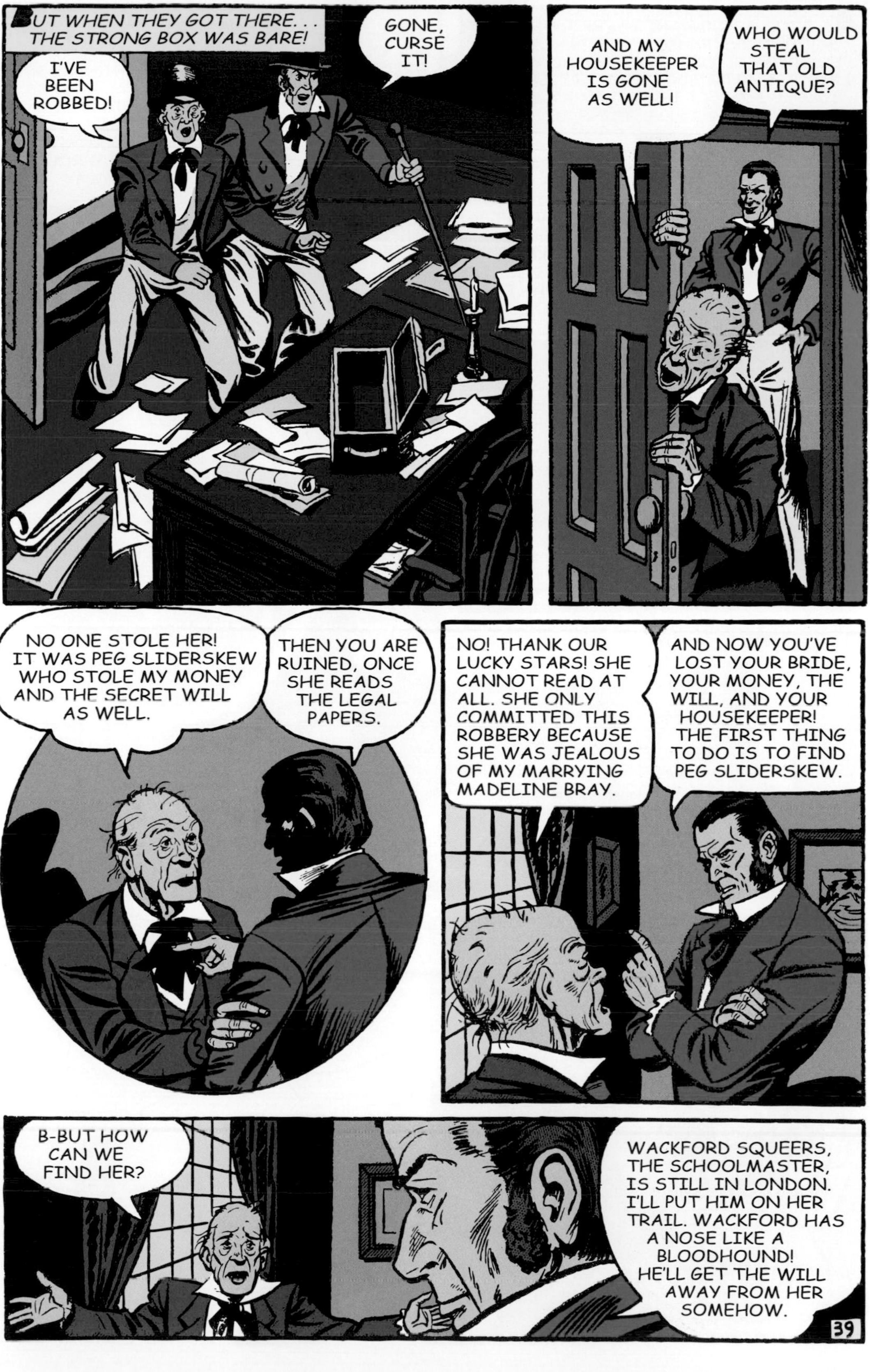
BUT WHEN THEY GOT THERE. . .
THE STRONG BOX WAS BARE!
I'VE BEEN ROBBED!
GONE, CURSE IT!
AND MY HOUSEKEEPER IS GONE AS WELL!
WHO WOULD STEAL THAT OLD ANTIQUE?
NO ONE STOLE HER! IT WAS PEG SLIDERSKEW WHO STOLE MY MONEY AND THE SECRET WILL AS WELL.
THEN YOU ARE RUINED, ONCE SHE READS THE LEGAL PAPERS.
NO! THANK OUR LUCKY STARS! SHE CANNOT READ AT ALL. SHE ONLY COMMITTED THIS ROBBERY BECAUSE SHE WAS JEALOUS OF MY MARRYING MADELINE BRAY.
AND NOW YOU'VE LOST YOUR BRIDE, YOUR MONEY, THE WILL, AND YOUR HOUSEKEEPER! THE FIRST THING TO DO IS TO FIND PEG SLIDERSKEW.
B-BUT HOW CAN WE FIND HER?
WACKFORD SQUEERS, THE SCHOOLMASTER, IS STILL IN LONDON. I'LL PUT HIM ON HER TRAIL. WACKFORD HAS A NOSE LIKE A BLOODHOUND! HE'LL GET THE WILL AWAY FROM HER SOMEHOW.
39

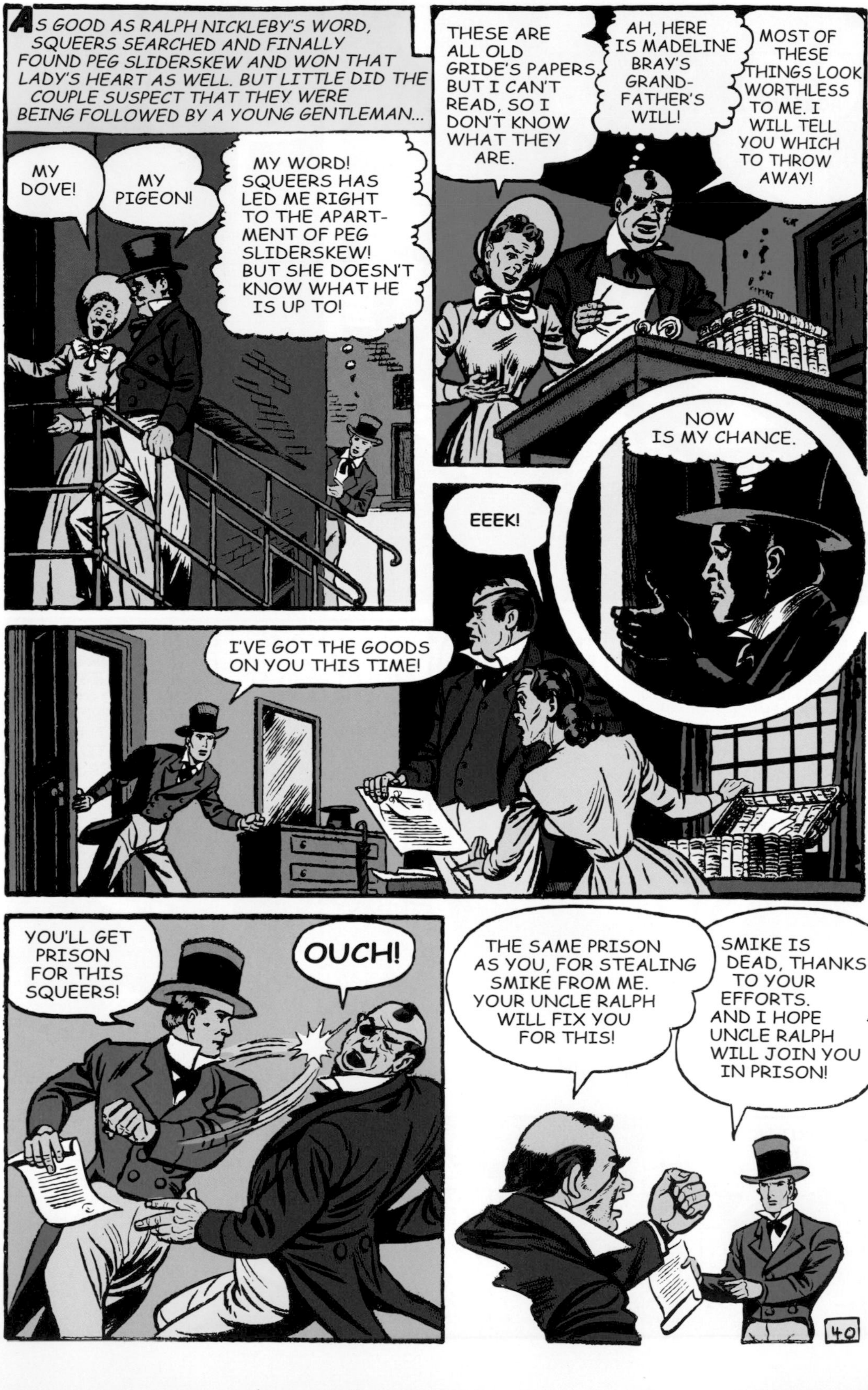
AS GOOD AS RALPH NICKLEBY'S WORD, SQUEERS SEARCHED AND FINALLY FOUND PEG SLIDERSKEW AND WON THAT LADY'S HEART AS WELL. BUT LITTLE DID THE COUPLE SUSPECT THAT THEY WERE BEING FOLLOWED BY A YOUNG GENTLEMAN...
MY DOVE!
MY PIGEON!
MY WORD! SQUEERS HAS LED ME RIGHT TO THE APARTMENT OF PEG SLIDERSKEW! BUT SHE DOESN'T KNOW WHAT HE IS UP TO!
THESE ARE ALL OLD GRIDE'S PAPERS, BUT I CAN'T READ, SO I DON'T KNOW WHAT THEY ARE.
AH, HERE IS MADELINE BRAY'S GRAND-FATHER'S WILL!
MOST OF THESE THINGS LOOK WORTHLESS TO ME. I WILL TELL YOU WHICH TO THROW AWAY!
NOW IS MY CHANCE.
EEEK!
I'VE GOT THE GOODS ON YOU THIS TIME!
YOU'LL GET PRISON FOR THIS SQUEERS!
OUCH!
THE SAME PRISON AS YOU, FOR STEALING SMIKE FROM ME. YOUR UNCLE RALPH WILL FIX YOU FOR THIS!
SMIKE IS DEAD, THANKS TO YOUR EFFORTS. AND I HOPE UNCLE RALPH WILL JOIN YOU IN PRISON!
40

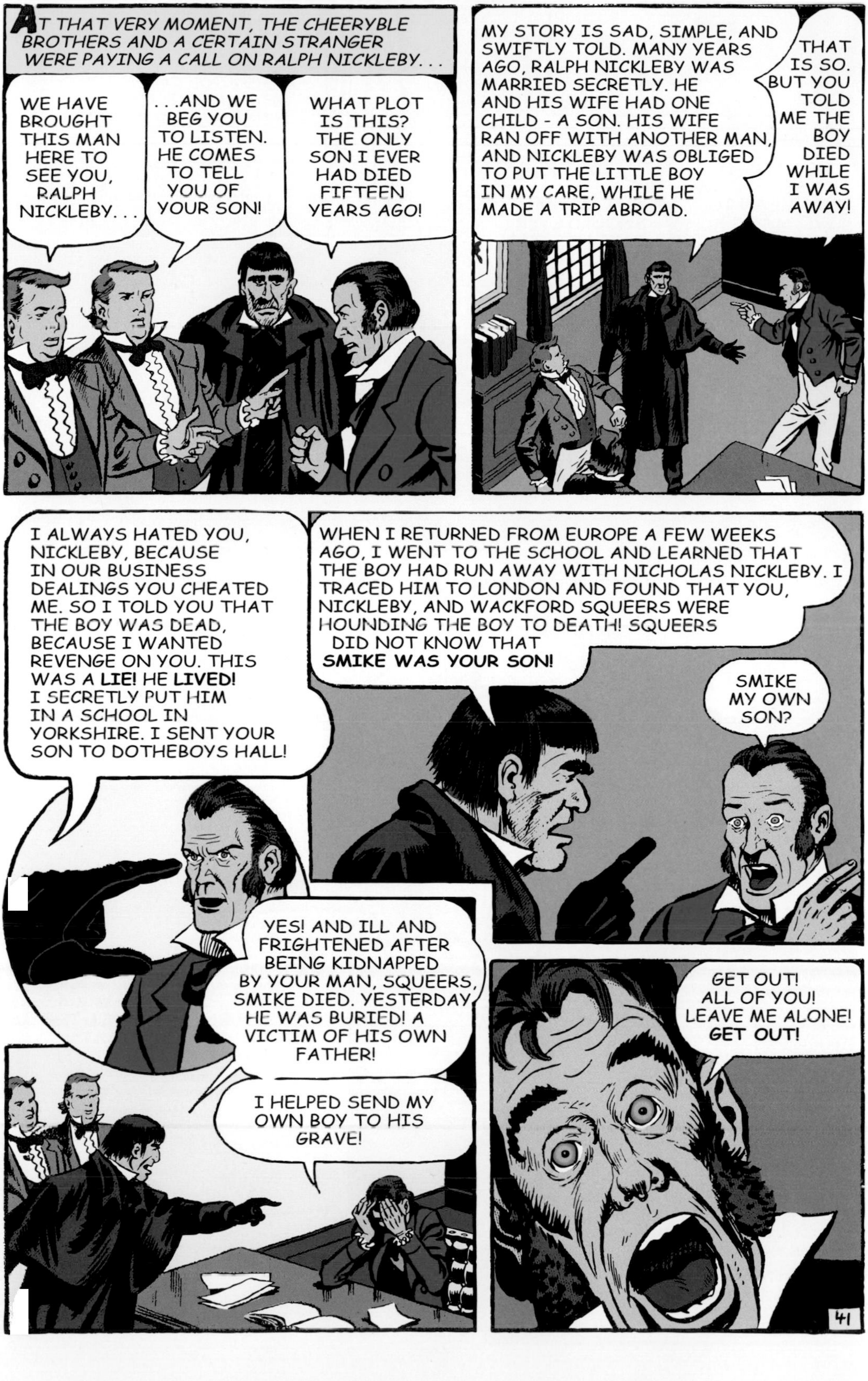
AT THAT VERY MOMENT, THE CHEERYBLE BROTHERS AND A CERTAIN STRANGER WERE PAYING A CALL ON RALPH NICKLEBY. . .
WE HAVE BROUGHT THIS MAN HERE TO SEE YOU, RALPH NICKLEBY. . .
. . .AND WE BEG YOU TO LISTEN. HE COMES TO TELL YOU OF YOUR SON!
WHAT PLOT IS THIS? THE ONLY SON I EVER HAD DIED FIFTEEN YEARS AGO!
MY STORY IS SAD, SIMPLE, AND SWIFTLY TOLD. MANY YEARS AGO, RALPH NICKLEBY WAS MARRIED SECRETLY. HE AND HIS WIFE HAD ONE CHILD - A SON. HIS WIFE RAN OFF WITH ANOTHER MAN, AND NICKLEBY WAS OBLIGED TO PUT THE LITTLE BOY IN MY CARE, WHILE HE MADE A TRIP ABROAD.
THAT IS SO. BUT YOU TOLD ME THE BOY DIED WHILE I WAS AWAY!
I ALWAYS HATED YOU, NICKLEBY, BECAUSE IN OUR BUSINESS DEALINGS YOU CHEATED ME. SO I TOLD YOU THAT THE BOY WAS DEAD, BECAUSE I WANTED REVENGE ON YOU. THIS WAS A **LIE!** HE **LIVED!** I SECRETLY PUT HIM IN A SCHOOL IN YORKSHIRE. I SENT YOUR SON TO DOTHEBOYS HALL!
WHEN I RETURNED FROM EUROPE A FEW WEEKS AGO, I WENT TO THE SCHOOL AND LEARNED THAT THE BOY HAD RUN AWAY WITH NICHOLAS NICKLEBY. I TRACED HIM TO LONDON AND FOUND THAT YOU, NICKLEBY, AND WACKFORD SQUEERS WERE HOUNDING THE BOY TO DEATH! SQUEERS DID NOT KNOW THAT **SMIKE WAS YOUR SON!**
SMIKE MY OWN SON?
YES! AND ILL AND FRIGHTENED AFTER BEING KIDNAPPED BY YOUR MAN, SQUEERS, SMIKE DIED. YESTERDAY HE WAS BURIED! A VICTIM OF HIS OWN FATHER!
I HELPED SEND MY OWN BOY TO HIS GRAVE!
GET OUT! ALL OF YOU! LEAVE ME ALONE! **GET OUT!**
41

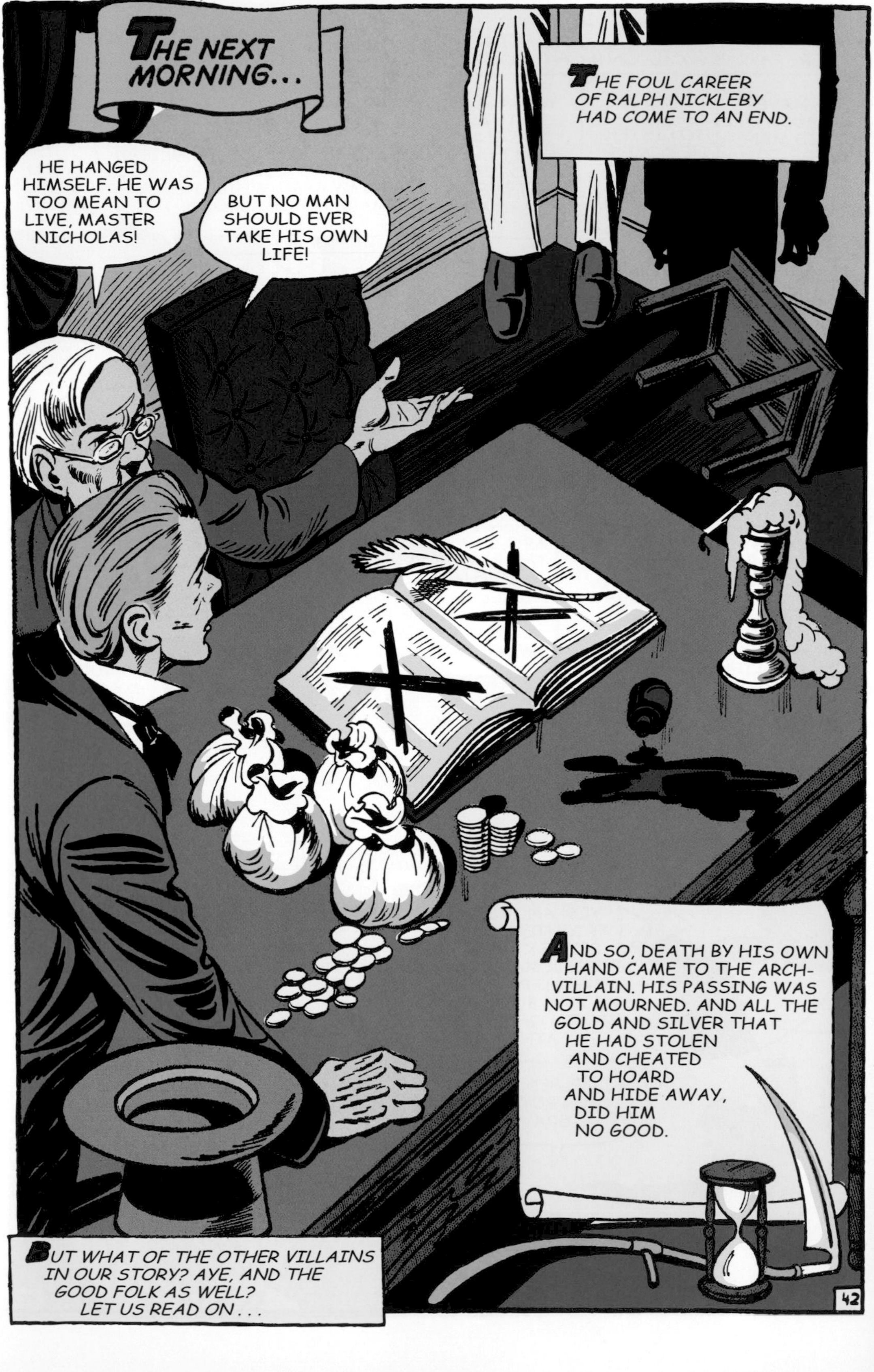
THE NEXT MORNING...
THE FOUL CAREER OF RALPH NICKLEBY HAD COME TO AN END.
HE HANGED HIMSELF. HE WAS TOO MEAN TO LIVE, MASTER NICHOLAS!
BUT NO MAN SHOULD EVER TAKE HIS OWN LIFE!
AND SO, DEATH BY HIS OWN HAND CAME TO THE ARCH-VILLAIN. HIS PASSING WAS NOT MOURNED. AND ALL THE GOLD AND SILVER THAT HE HAD STOLEN AND CHEATED TO HOARD AND HIDE AWAY, DID HIM NO GOOD.
BUT WHAT OF THE OTHER VILLAINS IN OUR STORY? AYE, AND THE GOOD FOLK AS WELL? LET US READ ON . . .
42

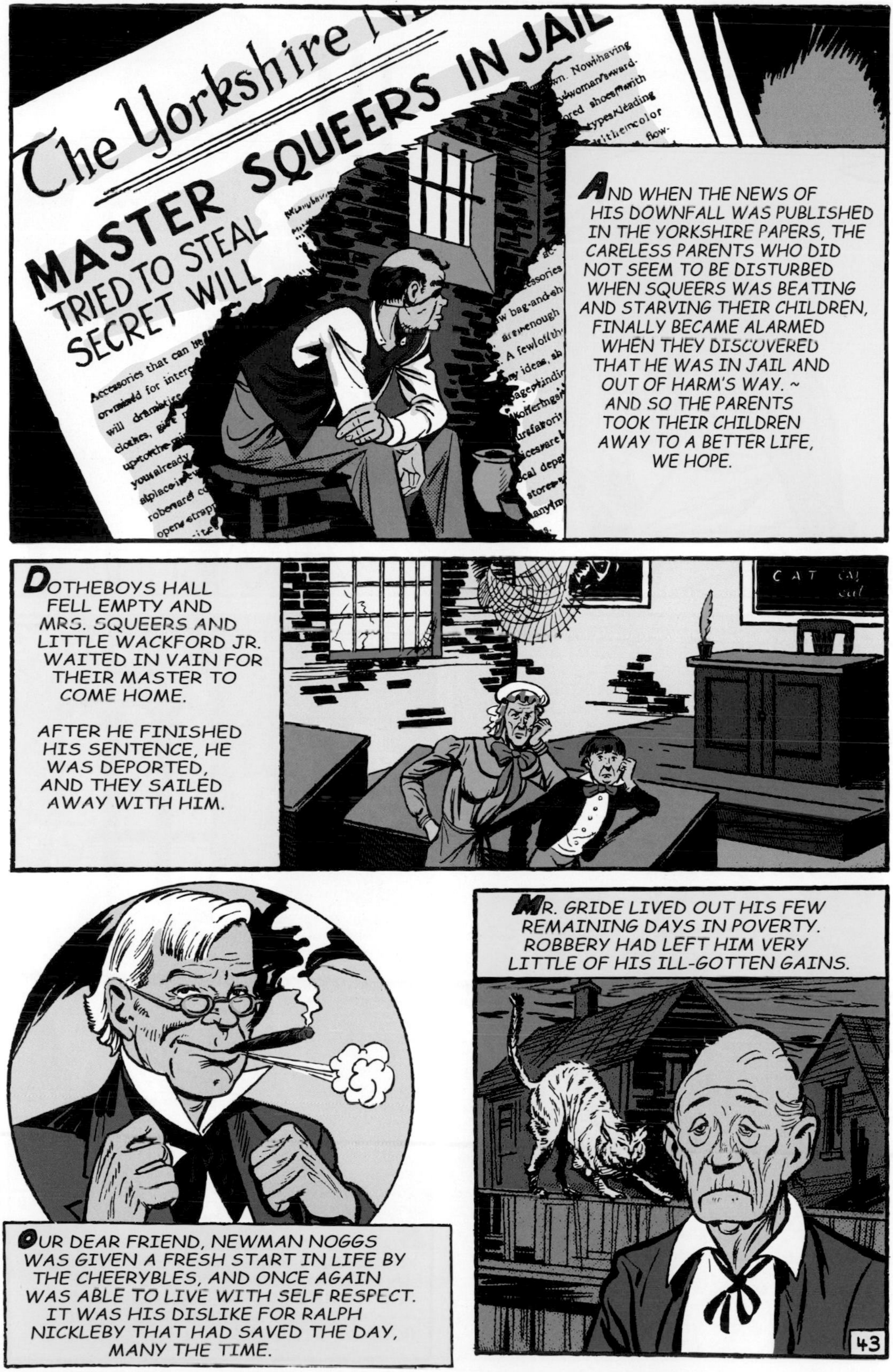
The Yorkshire N
MASTER SQUEERS IN JAIL
TRIED TO STEAL SECRET WILL
AND WHEN THE NEWS OF HIS DOWNFALL WAS PUBLISHED IN THE YORKSHIRE PAPERS, THE CARELESS PARENTS WHO DID NOT SEEM TO BE DISTURBED WHEN SQUEERS WAS BEATING AND STARVING THEIR CHILDREN, FINALLY BECAME ALARMED WHEN THEY DISCOVERED THAT HE WAS IN JAIL AND OUT OF HARM'S WAY. ~ AND SO THE PARENTS TOOK THEIR CHILDREN AWAY TO A BETTER LIFE, WE HOPE.
DOTHEBOYS HALL FELL EMPTY AND MRS. SQUEERS AND LITTLE WACKFORD JR. WAITED IN VAIN FOR THEIR MASTER TO COME HOME.
AFTER HE FINISHED HIS SENTENCE, HE WAS DEPORTED, AND THEY SAILED AWAY WITH HIM.
CAT
OUR DEAR FRIEND, NEWMAN NOGGS WAS GIVEN A FRESH START IN LIFE BY THE CHEERYBLES, AND ONCE AGAIN WAS ABLE TO LIVE WITH SELF RESPECT. IT WAS HIS DISLIKE FOR RALPH NICKLEBY THAT HAD SAVED THE DAY, MANY THE TIME.
MR. GRIDE LIVED OUT HIS FEW REMAINING DAYS IN POVERTY. ROBBERY HAD LEFT HIM VERY LITTLE OF HIS ILL-GOTTEN GAINS.
43

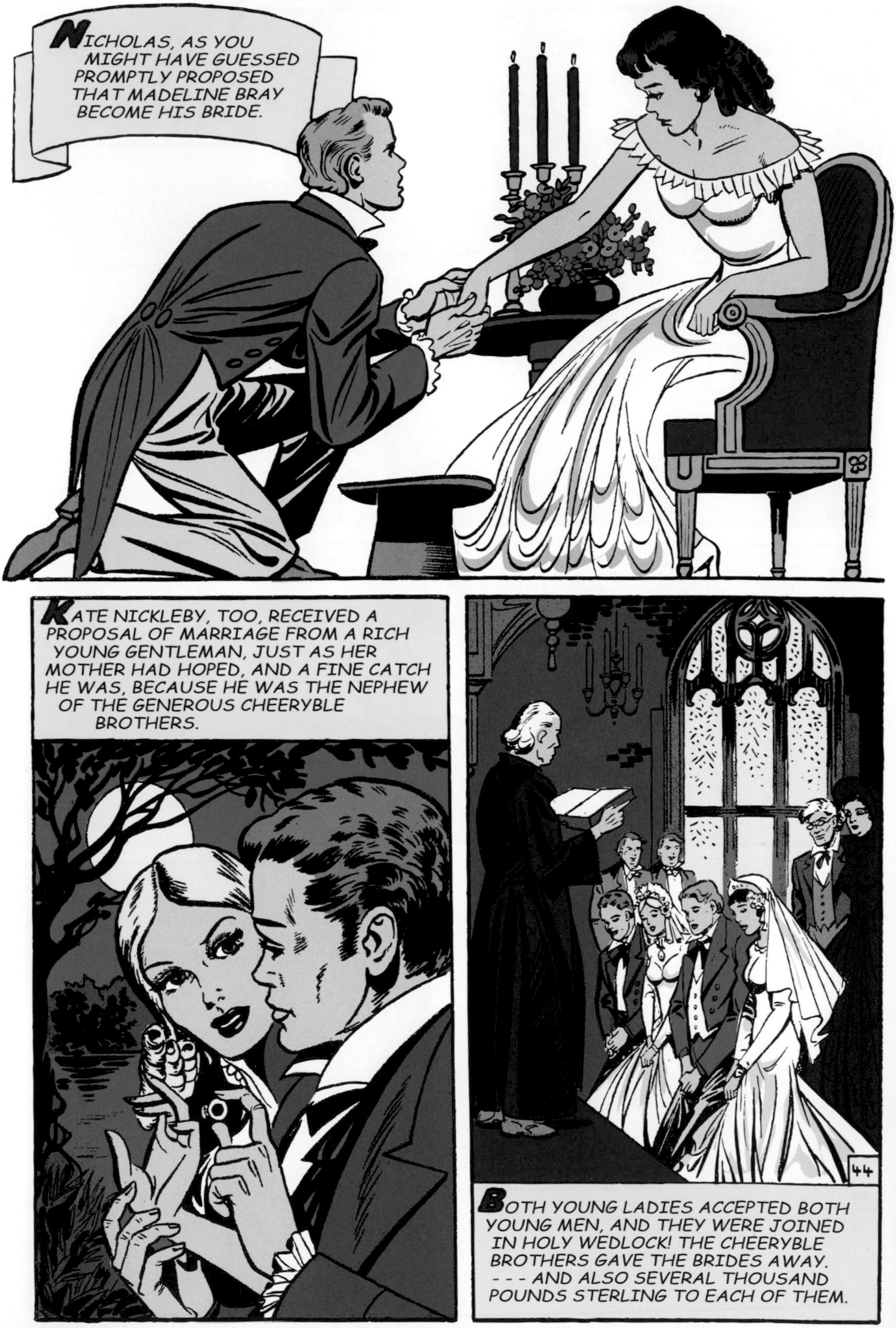
NICHOLAS, AS YOU MIGHT HAVE GUESSED PROMPTLY PROPOSED THAT MADELINE BRAY BECOME HIS BRIDE.
KATE NICKLEBY, TOO, RECEIVED A PROPOSAL OF MARRIAGE FROM A RICH YOUNG GENTLEMAN, JUST AS HER MOTHER HAD HOPED, AND A FINE CATCH HE WAS, BECAUSE HE WAS THE NEPHEW OF THE GENEROUS CHEERYBLE BROTHERS.
BOTH YOUNG LADIES ACCEPTED BOTH YOUNG MEN, AND THEY WERE JOINED IN HOLY WEDLOCK! THE CHEERYBLE BROTHERS GAVE THE BRIDES AWAY. - - - AND ALSO SEVERAL THOUSAND POUNDS STERLING TO EACH OF THEM.

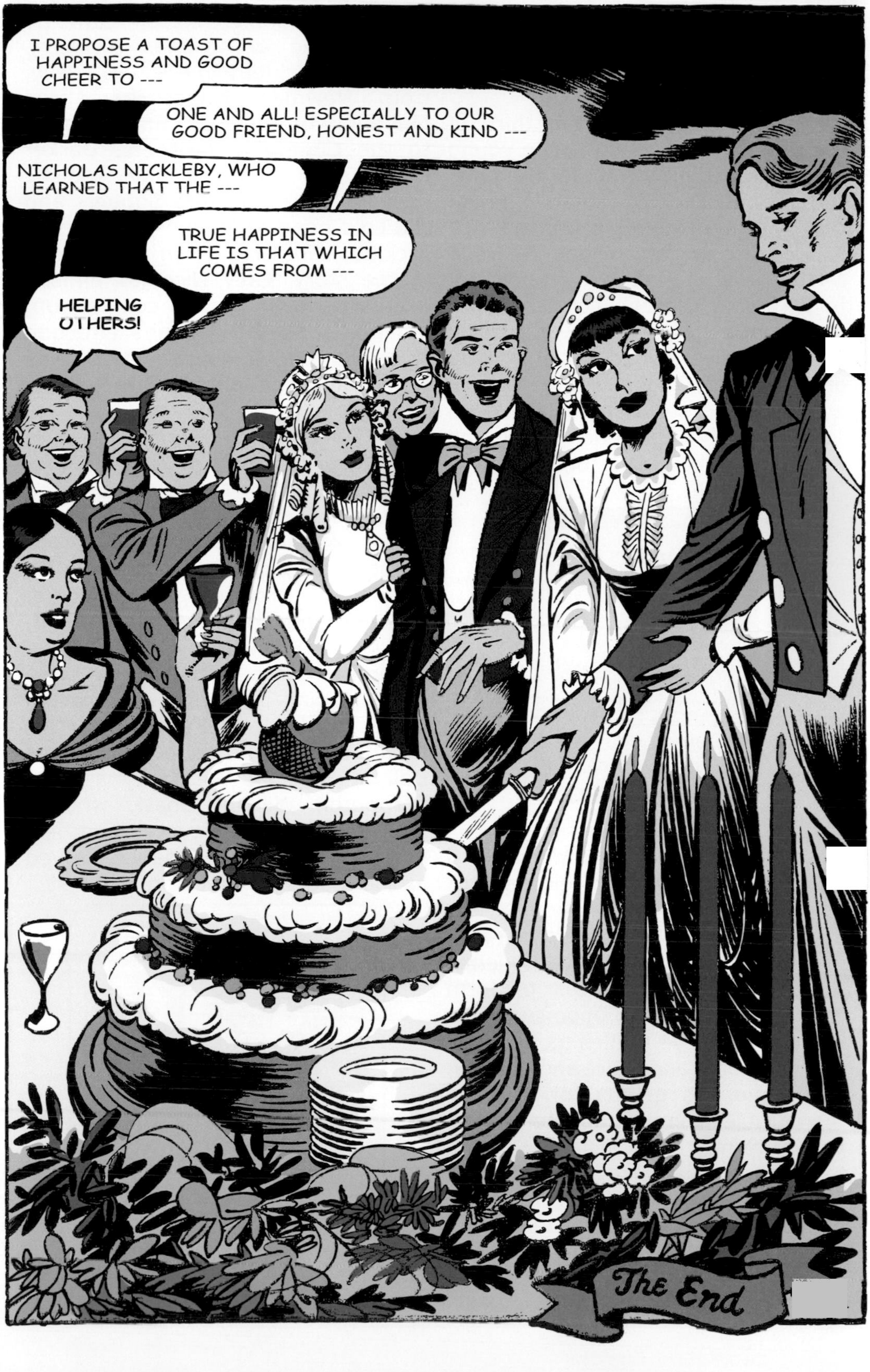
I PROPOSE A TOAST OF HAPPINESS AND GOOD CHEER TO ---
ONE AND ALL! ESPECIALLY TO OUR GOOD FRIEND, HONEST AND KIND ---
NICHOLAS NICKLEBY, WHO LEARNED THAT THE ---
TRUE HAPPINESS IN LIFE IS THAT WHICH COMES FROM ---
HELPING OTHERS!
The End

Nicholas Nickleby: Introduction

by William B. Jones, Jr.

Nicholas Nickleby was the third of Charles Dickens's novels. The young author signed a contract for the book with his publisher, Chapman and Hall, shortly after completing *The Pickwick Papers*. He began writing it when *Oliver Twist* was still in production. In *Nickleby*, Dickens combined the high comic spirits of his first novel with the impassioned social protest of his second. Originally appearing in a twenty-part serial from 31st March 1838 to 30th September 1839, the work was published in book form in October 1839.

Charles Dickens by Daniel Maclise (1839)

Structurally, *Nicholas Nickleby* owed much to the rambling eighteenth-century picaresque tradition of the author's beloved Henry Fielding (*Tom Jones*) and Tobias Smollett (*Roderick Random*). This looseness of form allowed Dickens the opportunity to explore narrative modes as different as melodrama and satire and, further, to indulge his genius for creating memorable comic characters. The very term "Dickensian" brings to mind a vast array of eccentric personalities whose driving force can often be reduced to one ruling passion, principle, or quirk.

A good number of these readily identifiable types can be found in *Nicholas Nickleby*, from Mrs. Nickleby to Miss La Creevy, from Newman Noggs to Alfred Mantolini, from the Crummles troupe to the Cheeryble brothers. Darker characters, such as the sadistic schoolmaster Wackford Squeers and the cold-hearted businessman Ralph Nickleby, are also given their scope in the story. Only Nicholas himself seems curiously flat in comparison, yet he earns the reader's affection through his unyielding devotion to his family and the unfortunate Smike.

Like *Oliver Twist*, which addressed the injustice of the Poor Law of 1834, *Nicholas Nickleby* targeted a specific social evil: the brutality of the infamous Yorkshire boarding schools, which later figured in Charlotte Bronte's *Jane Eyre*. Dickens and his illustrator friend, Hablôt K. Browne ("Phiz"), visited several of these institutions in early 1838, paying particular attention to Bowes Academy at Greta Bridge. This notorious school inspired Dotheboys Hall in *Nicholas Nickleby*, and its proprietor, William Shaw, who in 1823 had been prosecuted and held liable for criminal negligence, served as the model for Wackford Squeers.

The Internal Economy of Dotheboys Hall (Phiz, 1838)

The impact of Dickens's novel on the institution of the squalid **Cont'd**

Yorkshire schools was decisive. By the time he penned his preface to an 1848 edition of *Nicholas Nickleby*, ten years after he began researching and writing the book, he was able to announce that "There were, then, a good many cheap Yorkshire schools in existence. There are very few now." Such was the weight of Dickens's moral authority and the power of his art. Yet *Nicholas Nickleby* is, above all, a celebration of the amplitude of human experience, given symbolic affirmation in the final chapter's account of the double wedding and the children's care for the "dead boy's grave."

Mr. Ralph Nickleby's Honest Composure (Phiz, 1838)

From the beginning, the novel has been popular with readers, though not with critics. It has been staged more than 250 times and adapted for film or television at least ten times since 1903. The most acclaimed theatrical production was the Royal Shakespeare Company's West End and Broadway success (1980, 1981), which had a playing time of more than eight hours and featured a large ensemble cast in multiple roles. In 1982, a television recording of the play was broadcast. The first sound film version, starring Sir Cedric Hardwicke, was released in 1947, when a postwar revival of interest in the works of Dickens was in full swing. More recently, an all-star cast headed by Christopher Plummer appeared in a colourful 2002 cinematic treatment.

In November 1950, Seaboard Publishers' "Stories by Famous Authors Illustrated" series issued an adaptation of *Nicholas Nickleby* as No. 9 in the comic book series (which had initially been styled "Fast Fiction"). The Dickens story was illustrated by Gustav Schrotter, a children's book artist who would later supply covers and interiors for Seaboard editions of Lew Wallace's *Ben-Hur* and George du Maurier's *Trilby* (retitled *La Svengali*). Scripted by Dick Davis, the Famous Authors 45-page rendering of *Nicholas Nickleby* was largely faithful. Although certain characters and episodes were necessarily omitted and the fate of Arthur Gride softened, the adaptation on the whole buoyantly conveyed the energy of the Dickens novel.

Albert L. Kanter, owner of the Gilberton Company's *Classics Illustrated* series, had been carefully watching the competing Famous Authors line since its launching in 1949. (A principal CI artist, Henry C. Kiefer, also supplied art for nine Famous Authors titles.) Upon the release of Famous Authors No. 13, Rafael Sabatini's *Scaramouche*, in March 1951, Kanter bought the publication outright and discontinued it, turning the scheduled issue No. 14, Stephen Crane's *The Red Badge of Courage*, into Classics *Illustrated* No. 98 (August 1952). *The Red Badge* artist was none other than Gustav Schrotter, who had also contributed to Iger Shop teamwork on Classics *Illustrated* No. 65, *Benjamin Franklin* (November 1949), and No. 88, Howard Pyle's *Men of Iron* (October 1951).

Cont'd

Classic Comic Store has now added the Famous Authors edition of *Nicholas Nickleby* to the Classics *Illustrated* series as issue No. 32, the first new title in the 48 page series since the 1969 publication of No. 169, *Negro Americans: The Early Years*.

A TREASURY OF
CELEBRATED LITERATURE
No 9
AUTHORS
Nicholas Nickleby
by CHARLES DICKENS
10¢

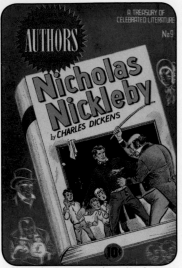

Stories by Famous Authors, No. 9 - *Nicholas Nickleby* (1950)

Nicholas Nickleby retains the 1950 Schrotter interior art and offers a newly commissioned gouache cover by Colin Mayne that alludes to the earlier Famous Authors line-drawn cover (see picture above). With the inclusion of this work, the new Classics *Illustrated* catalogue will now contain six masterpieces by "the inimitable Boz": No. 2, *Oliver Twist*; No. 15, *A Christmas Carol*; No. 20, *Great Expectations*; No. 32, *Nicholas Nickleby*; No. 35, *A Tale of Two Cities* and No. 40, *David Copperfield*.

Nicholas Nickleby at the Movies

The first screen adaptation of the book was in 1903 – and was known in the UK as *Dotheboys Hall: or, Nicholas Nickleby*. This was followed in 1912 with a 20 minute adaptation directed by George Nichols. This film is available on DVD in the British Film Institute's compendium release "Dickens Before Sound". It is well thought of by film critics allowing for the cinematic limitations of the time.

In 1947 Alberto Cavalcanti directed an ambitious film version of the book entitled *The Life and Adventures of Nicholas Nickleby*. Derek Bond played Nicholas and Cedric Hardwicke played Ralph. This was a very high quality production but it probably suffered when compared against David Lean's higher profile cinematic adaptations of *Great Expectations* with John Mills and *Oliver Twist* with Alec Guinness.

A ten episode TV series was broadcast in 1957 by the BBC and the Corporation adapted the book again in 1968 with Martin Jarvis in the lead role. The "Beeb" returned to the book in 1977 with Nigel Havers in the title role in a lavish 6 episode series. TV channels clearly saw the potential to serialise the book and Channel Four adapted it in 1982 in two parts. In 1985 an Australian company released a 72 minute animated version of the story. Movie Producers were at it again in 2001 with a well acclaimed version starring James D'arcy in the title role.

A worldwide release in 2002 with a star studded cast including Christopher Plummer, Tom Courtenay and Anne Hathaway received much worldwide acclaim. Clearly the plot lends itself to the TV and Movie screen – something Dickens could not have anticipated - and we can expect regular adaptations of the tale – simply because it relates the story of triumph against hardship and love shining through against mean-spiritedness and cruelty.